ALPHA SQUAD

INFILTRATOR

LORELEI MOONE

eXplicitTales

CONTENTS

PROLOGUE

SIX MONTHS AGO

"Thomas," Eric Blackwood, alpha of the Wolf settlement in Rannoch, Scotland, spoke in a low but determined voice.

"Yes, Alpha." Thomas Blackwood averted his gaze, as was customary when the pack leader addressed an underling.

"As you know, since the emergence of the New Alliance and the exposure of our kind to the world, we've been trailing behind the rest of shifterkind in our efforts to come to terms with the new reality. Now that the human government is starting some kind of law enforcement program with the New Alliance, we cannot afford to remain complacent any longer. We must act!"

Thomas blinked a few times. *Where was this conversation headed?* "I agree, Sir."

"What would you say if I asked you to join this new initiative? To be our eyes and ears within this… what is it called again?"

"Alpha Squad, Sir."

Alpha Blackwood scoffed. "That's right. *Alpha* Squad. I've managed to pull a few strings and get you inserted into their training program. The rest is up to you. Failure is not an option; our pack relies on you."

Thomas took a deep breath and nodded solemnly. He would not let down his alpha, or the rest of the pack. It was a great honor to be chosen for a mission such as this, and he would never forgive himself if he messed it up.

Plus, this would be the first time he'd actually move out of Rannoch. It was a chance unlike any other to see what the rest of the world was like, and he was keen to learn everything he could.

"A lot rests on your shoulders, but I wouldn't have chosen you for the job unless I thought you could hack it," the alpha said. "It's a delicate matter, and you'll understand that I prefer to keep things in the family for now…"

Thomas nodded again. Ever since Alpha Blackwood had sent his very own daughter to Edinburgh to work with the Alliance about a year ago, there weren't any other Blackwoods in the pack to take on a job like this. Thomas, being the alpha's nephew, was a logical choice. More so since Thomas's very own parents had passed away a few years back and the alpha and his wife had taken a special interest in his education and upbringing. He owed his aunt and uncle a lot, and now the time had come for him to repay them.

"Thank you, Sir. I will do my best."

The alpha rested his hand on Thomas's shoulder.

Even though his hair was starting to grey around his temples, Alpha Blackwood was an impressive looking man. His large, strong hand weighed heavy on Thomas's shoulder, even though the younger wolf was no weakling himself.

"The physical training should not challenge you too much. Focus your energy on making the others trust you. They must never suspect that you report to me."

"No problem," Thomas said firmly, even though the prospect of having to deceive fellow trainees and the squad's leadership was a worrying one. He wasn't a liar by nature.

But if his alpha commanded it, he had to obey. That was how wolf society worked.

"Good. Training begins on Monday. Pack up your things and someone will take you to the train station later today. All the arrangements have been made."

Thomas swallowed hard. *Later today?*

He'd been around when Heidi, his cousin, left for Edinburgh last year. He'd heard the rumors of how the whole thing went down and even watched as she got into one of the pack's Jeeps, never to be seen again. She hadn't had any more notice than this, so how could he expect anything different for himself? He wasn't even the alpha's direct offspring.

So he didn't argue, and did what he was told.

Packing did not take long. Even so, he didn't have much time for goodbyes.

He didn't permit himself to think or analyze the situation too much. These were his orders, and he would follow them to the best of his abilities.

Only when he found himself alone on the train later in the day did he take a short breather.

How strange, leaving Rannoch. Heidi had never come back home and although rumors were plentiful, Thomas had no real idea why her departure had been permanent.

Was it by choice? Had something happened to her out here?

The world outside of Rannoch was a big place. Perhaps she'd been ill-equipped to deal with it all and gotten herself into trouble. They were cousins, and not too far apart in age, but they'd never been close. Still, he couldn't help but wonder what might've happened to her.

And what would become of him? Would he be successful? Would he be able to keep his true orders under wraps and fool his fellow recruits?

What would happen if he was found out?

His train came to a halt in a quiet station and he observed a tearful reunion outside on the platform. A young couple, overjoyed to see each other again.

Perhaps the outside world wasn't all bad. He'd stood by and watched as some of his peers had paired up around him within Rannoch itself. But he'd never felt any attraction or pull toward any of the she-wolves in his age group.

This mission into the great unknown might make him cross paths with his own mate. He certainly hoped so.

She had to be out there somewhere; he just hadn't met her yet...

CHAPTER ONE

These past few months, Private Jill Callahan had been the happiest she'd ever been in her professional life, as well as the most troubled.

Alpha Squad was a tough assignment, no doubt. And although the squad had gotten off to a difficult start, with each passing mission, they seemed to work just a little bit better together.

This was a career changer for her.

A chance to be part of something completely new and meaningful.

Jill wouldn't give it up for the world.

And yet, every night when she went to bed, sleep eluded her.

Every morning before it was time to get up, she found that she was already awake and staring at the ceiling in the dark.

She saw herself as the quiet backbone of the squad. Making travel arrangements, answering phone calls, setting up meetings, and completing necessary paperwork. She wasn't actively involved in the missions; she didn't investigate crimes or chase down troublemakers, usually. But without her, things wouldn't run nearly as smoothly.

She wasn't as important as Major Janine Williams, who ran the squad, but her work was imperative to the smooth running of everyday affairs. If she let things slip, everyone would feel the effects.

So why couldn't she just relax and allow herself some proper rest once her daily duties were over?

In one word: Blackwood.

The only wolf on the squad, recruit Blackwood had turned her world upside down. She had no idea why; the two had barely had a proper conversation in all the time they'd spent together both on-base and in the field. She liked to think that she wasn't so shallow that she'd lust after the man simply because he was hot.

Though he was.

Objectively speaking, all the recruits were fine specimens of the opposite sex, though Jill did not like to think of them that way. But at times like these, with hours to go before dawn, these were the thoughts that occupied her mind.

Throughout her career in the military, she had been surrounded by fit men. But only one had only ever affected her so deeply.

Blackwood.

She didn't even know the man, not really. She knew he was a wolf shifter, and that he was from a town in Scotland which she'd never heard of before. She also knew about his stellar performance during boot camp, of course; she'd typed up his reports, after all.

But despite sneaking the occasional peek at his dossier,

she did not know *who he really was.*

How could she feel so connected to a complete stranger?

A complete stranger with perfect washboard abs and a boyish smile that could melt even the coldest of hearts.

Either way, Jill wasn't in the habit of mixing work and pleasure. Her irrational attraction to Thomas Blackwood had made her avoid him completely. In the military, it would've been against the rules to fraternize within the same squad. Although Alpha Squad played by its own rules which had not been so strictly defined yet, just the thought of starting a relationship with Blackwood went against Jill's own code of conduct.

She couldn't imagine doing such a thing.

What Major Williams had going on with Eric King was her own business.

Their affair had begun sometime during boot camp itself. Jill did her best not to judge, but she certainly wouldn't have started anything if she was in the major's position.

Way too much scrutiny.

And Eric King's appointment as second-in-command could easily be interpreted as favoritism by those in the know. Luckily, nobody else on the team seemed any the wiser.

Still, none of these idle thoughts helped her figure out a way to resolve her own problem. How was she going to keep ignoring Thomas Blackwood when he was so annoyingly present every day they worked together?

From boot camp, which saw them all living on base together, and even heading out into the wilderness for training exercises. To their first mission in Sevenoaks, during which they all occupied the same quaint little country inn.

There had been a couple more such missions. Now that shifters were fully integrating into human society, there was always some incident or some investigation that could benefit from the expertise offered by Alpha Squad.

Their political ally and self-appointed superior, Secretary of Shifter Affairs Oliver Teese, had sent the squad into various towns all over the country. They weren't always welcome—at least not at first—but they'd managed to create a reputation for themselves as a task force that did the job with minimum fuss and drama, and maximum results.

So why was it so hard for Jill to focus on the job, and the job alone? How long would she have to suffer in silence until her fixation on Blackwood would pass and she could get on with her life again?

The shrill sound of her alarm interrupted her deep thoughts and spurred her into action.

She tried to shake off the fatigue that lingered in her tired limbs and force herself into a more productive state of mind.

It was another day, and she would bring her all to the

job.

While suffering in silence every time Blackwood came near.

She shook off any lingering thoughts about him and got up, ready to start her daily routine.

———◆———

"Are we all set for recruit McMillan's arrival?" Major Williams asked.

Jill nodded. "Yes, Ma'am. The new quarters have plenty of room. I've prepared one unit for McMillan."

The major folded her hands on her desk. "Wonderful. I'm sure he'll be a valuable addition to the team."

"I agree." Jill lingered inside the office for a bit, wondering if she could leave yet, when the major started to speak again.

"Say, I apologize if I'm in the wrong here, but is something troubling you?" Major Williams cocked her head to the side as she observed Jill.

Jill swallowed hard and shook her head. "Just tired, Ma'am."

Major Williams nodded. "It's been a busy few months. If there's more to it, or if you need some time off, please do let me know."

Jill pressed her lips together. They were the only two women on this part of the base, so the temptation to open up was there, but they weren't equals. No way could she confide in Major Williams with her personal issues.

"Everything is fine, Major."

"Very well. You are dismissed. Please inform me when recruit McMillan arrives on base."

"Yes, Ma'am."

Jill turned on her heel and left the major's office. That was a close call. She passed Eric King on the way through the hallway. She nodded at him, a greeting which he reciprocated without slowing down or pausing. Clearly, the man was in a hurry.

She shrugged and headed straight for her office. Despite the rough start to this morning, she still had plenty of work to get on with. Sure, McMillan's room was prepared and ready, but his paperwork was not.

Jill sunk into her chair and organized the scattered papers on her desk. Sleep deprivation made it difficult to focus. Her response to Major Williams' questions had mostly been correct. She *was* tired. Exhausted, actually. But she didn't have time to dwell on that.

Instead of wasting any more of her morning, Jill picked up the phone for one of the more annoying jobs of the day.

"Hello? Private Callahan calling from Alpha Squad. Could you put me through to General Stone's office, please?" Jill asked.

The line went silent for a moment.

"General Stone's office, Private Fairweather speaking," a female voice answered.

Jill rested her head in her hand, which also held the receiver, and closed her eyes.

"Morning, Fairweather. I was just checking on the status of those gate passes for our new recruit."

"Name?"

Jill rolled her eyes. Fairweather knew exactly who she was talking about. This was the first new recruit they'd brought on since the beginning of Alpha Squad several months ago.

"McMillan, Sean."

Rustling of papers could be heard on the other end of the line. Jill pinched the bridge of her nose as she waited. Of all the irritating side-effects of her sleep troubles, headaches were the worst.

"I'm afraid I'm going to need more time for those. It looks like General Stone has not yet signed off."

"The recruit is arriving today. We're going to need these passes quite soon," Jill said. Despite running on half-empty, she was still much more efficient than anyone else she had the misfortune of dealing with on this base. It was due to General Stone's disapproval of Alpha Squad as a whole; that much was clear. He was doing his utmost to hold up anything he could.

Perhaps the aim was to frustrate the squad out of existence?

"I see, but these things cannot be rushed, you understand. We have to follow protocol." Fairweather sounded flat and disinterested as usual, with a hint of cockiness that rubbed Jill the wrong way.

It was tempting to lose her cool, to tell the woman exactly what she thought of her phone manner as well as General Stone's petty games. But Jill kept her opinions to herself.

Fairweather had her orders, just as Jill did. The two of them were just pawns in the idiotic power struggle between Major Williams and General Stone.

But Jill was nothing if not patient and professional. Only if her repeated efforts remained unsuccessful would she involve the major in this mess. Once she did, chances were that one phone call from her to Secretary Teese would resolve the entire matter instantly. But that was a short cut. She was determined to try for a solution herself first.

"Okay, well, I'll call back in a few days then," Jill said. "Thank you *so* much for your help."

"Happy Easter!" Fairweather ended the call.

"Happy Easter, indeed," Jill grumbled to herself, still holding the receiver in her hands. What kind of a person wished people Happy Easter in advance, during Lent? She was convinced Private Fairweather had only said it to annoy her.

After putting the phone down, Jill tried to focus on another one of her daily tasks. She opened the websites for all major newspapers, on the lookout not just for any mention of Alpha Squad, but any story with shifter involvement. They'd been stuck on base for the better part of two weeks. A new mission would be a welcome change of routine.

Just as she'd worked her way through the first paper, her phone rang.

"Alpha Squad, Major Williams' office, this is Private Callahan speaking," Jill answered almost on autopilot.

"Secretary Teese for Major Williams," a male voice announced. It wasn't the secretary himself, of course, but one of his office staff.

Jill quickly checked her calendar. No, there was no briefing scheduled for today. *Wonder what he wants?*

"Just a moment, please," Jill said, before dialing through to the major's office. "Ma'am, you have a call from Secretary Teese."

"Put him through," Major Williams said.

Jill did as asked, and sat back in her chair as she listened in on the conversation that followed.

CHAPTER TWO

Thomas Blackwood had started his day bright and early. He had a spring in his step and a boatload of energy and excitement fueling him. It was the end of March and spring had finally sprung, though that wasn't the reason he was pumped.

Today was a significant day, in a way. It felt a bit silly to acknowledge it out loud—the guys would no doubt make fun of him if he did—so he'd kept it to himself.

It was Alpha Squad's six month anniversary.

The squad had been through a few ups and downs together, but they'd always come out on top. He was proud to be a part of it.

Sure, he was technically working for a different master, but it hadn't interfered with his team duties at all. Alpha Blackwood had wanted reports on the squad's various missions, and he'd provided them.

No harm, no foul.

Better yet, after a slightly rough start, which saw the humans and shifters on the team pitched against one another, they'd begun to work together better and better with each deployment. He'd started to develop a kind of kinship with the other team members; he'd begun to trust them like he did members of his own clan back in Rannoch.

This morning was special in another way too. Today, they'd welcome another recruit onto the team. Sean McMillan, the human/bear shifter hybrid who'd helped the squad out in Sevenoaks some months back.

Negotiations had taken a while, but Major Williams had finally managed to convince the man to join their ranks. Although technically wolves and bears were natural enemies, Thomas had never really understood the basis of this centuries old rivalry. He certainly didn't jump to conclusions or judge people by their species. Another team member was a positive as far as he was concerned, no matter his origins.

And as such, he was excited for the newcomer's arrival, perhaps more so than any of the other guys.

Really, there was just one factor which could dampen his mood this morning and that was even more embarrassing to admit than any of this other stuff combined.

Private Callahan.

The petite and quiet assistant to Major Williams was a constant influence on his mood. He couldn't explain quite how it worked, but every time Thomas caught a glimpse of her, his heart sang. If she inadvertently looked in his direction, his nerves surged.

If by chance she failed to cross paths with him on any given day, his day was essentially ruined.

He'd admired her from afar ever since his arrival on base all those months ago. It was a bit creepy, how fixated he was on her. Like a stalker, he watched out for her, and often caught himself when his eyes lingered on her just a bit too long for comfort.

At least nobody had suspected anything, except maybe the object of his desire herself.

Private Callahan had barely spoken a word to him in six months. She made sure never to come too near or be alone with him. Whenever he was around, she seemed to act as though he was infected with a dangerous disease. She wasn't all wrong, of course. Even though she was only human, her instincts had picked up on his obsession and as a result, she was always on defense with him.

He wasn't sure whether to be impressed by her keen intuition or feel slighted.

Still, no matter how frustrated he sometimes became by her standoffish behavior, he could not hold it against her for long. She remained ever-perfect; a brunette goddess without a single flaw. In his mind, she could do no wrong; it was him who was at fault. He'd brought all of this on himself by acting like a complete tool around her.

"Blackwood, report to Major Williams' office," a stern voice interrupted his thoughts. He looked up to find Eric King, the major's second-in-command, staring at him with his arms folded.

"I'll be right there," Thomas mumbled, while avoiding eye contact with the bear shifter, as was wolf custom when addressed by one's superiors.

For but a split second, he wondered what the major wanted to see him about. The second and much more pressing thing on his mind was whether Private Callahan would be in Major Williams' office. He hoped so.

———•◦•———

Thomas did his best to listen to the Major's orders, though his thoughts might as well have been miles away. Private Callahan's absence had his thoughts tied up in loops.

"The evidence does seem to point at wolf involvement," Major Williams concluded.

Thomas blinked a few times. *What had she just said?*

"Are you still with me, soldier?"

"I apologize, Ma'am. Yes indeed, wolf involvement. We ought to investigate this matter as soon as possible," Thomas agreed, even though he was still a little fuzzy on the details. Apparently there had been a string of thefts somewhere up north. He wasn't clear on why any of his kin would bother with petty crimes like that, but he was in no position to argue. The information about the case had come directly from the Ministry of Shifter Affairs.

"Since recruit McMillan is arriving today, and it's important he undergoes training as normal, we'll split up the squad," Major Williams continued.

Thomas's heart skipped a few beats. If he was to go investigate those thefts with half the squad, was Private Callahan going to accompany them or would she stay on base? He hoped for the former possibility, obviously. Just the thought of spending time away from her…

He took a deep breath and tried to focus on not sounding like an idiot in front of the Major.

"Who all will travel off base?"

The Major studied his face for a moment, which was awkward.

"I haven't decided yet. Once McMillan gets here we'll do a squad briefing."

"Yes, Ma'am. Very good," Thomas mumbled.

When he found her still staring at him, he forced himself into action and left the office.

Now what? He only had partial information relating to Alpha Squad's new mission, but the potential involvement of a pack of lawless wolves made it exactly the sort of thing worth reporting back home.

He was halfway down the hall when Adam King, the second bear shifter on the squad and Eric's brother, came up behind him and slapped him on the back. "What's this I hear about a new mission?" he asked.

Thomas shrugged, conscious of the heavy weight of Adam's arm still resting on his shoulder. "The Major will brief us once McMillan gets here."

"Aha. Well, it would be good to get out of here for a while." Adam shot him a smile.

"Mhm," Thomas responded. He wasn't so sure about that. Not unless Private Callahan accompanied them. If she didn't, it was a disaster as far as he was concerned.

"Cool, well, I can't wait for the briefing. I'm going a bit stir crazy being confined to base," Adam said.

"Right," Thomas said.

Adam gave him a sideways look and shrugged before heading back toward the exit. Thomas continued on to his quarters. Alpha Squad accommodations had greatly improved in the six months they'd been here. They'd started with a single dorm room for everyone, but slowly and steadily, renovations were carried out in the barracks so that each team member had a room of their own.

Especially on days like today, Thomas was glad to have the additional privacy.

He locked the door behind himself and switched on his phone. His sense of duty had prevailed. He had to inform his alpha of the upcoming mission, even if his understanding of it was limited.

The phone rang only a couple of times before the alpha's wife and Thomas's aunt, Rebecca Blackwood, answered.

"Hello?"

"This is Thomas. I have news for the alpha."

"Is everything alright, son? You sound a bit bleak. Have you been getting enough sleep?"

The barrage of concerned questions made Thomas smile. It was wholly unnecessary, but he enjoyed when his aunt fussed over him like that.

"Of course, Aunt Rebecca. I'm good."

"Who is it?" a male voice asked in the background.

"It's Thomas. He has news for you." Aunt Rebecca's voice was hushed, but Thomas could still hear her clearly.

Thomas waited patiently for the phone receiver to be passed across.

"Yes, Thomas? What have you got to report?"

"Alpha Squad has a new mission. A string of thefts up north. The Ministry of Shifter Affairs has received reports of wolf activity in the area and they suspect that wolves may be involved in the crimes."

"Really? What an outrageous accusation! This is unacceptable. Thomas, you must take control of the situation and ensure these lies don't spread any further!"

Thomas swallowed hard. He'd expected Alpha Blackwood to disapprove of this mission, but he hadn't counted on this much rage.

"Of course we will get to the bottom of it. The truth—" Thomas started.

"Nonsense! They will use this to drag our reputation through the mud! These humans will turn the tide against us. And don't forget you're the only one of us on the team. The bears and the humans will conspire with one another to make us wolves look bad!"

Thomas frowned. He'd always gotten along with everyone on the team, Eric and Adam included. Species seemed to not factor into it. The three of them were working hard to help all shifters, not just their own kind. If anything, the shifters felt a kinship with one another which they did not share with the humans on the team.

"I have made my wishes very clear," the alpha spoke in a low growl. "Do you understand, Thomas?"

"Yes, Alpha," Thomas said.

He disagreed with his uncle's assessment of the situation, but there was nothing he could do. Orders were orders. He would not tolerate backtalk or arguing, especially not at a time when tensions ran so high. A wolf simply did not disobey his alpha, except if he sought to overthrow him and take his place. Thomas had no desire to do anything like that.

"Then you'll do as instructed. You'll stop this investigation by any means necessary."

Thomas closed his eyes and tried to think of a way out. There was none.

"Yes, Alpha," he whispered.

The line went silent, and Thomas found himself with the phone still in his hand, staring into empty space. What on earth was he supposed to do?

On the one hand, Major Williams expected his full involvement in this mission, and on the other hand, his alpha demanded he kill the entire thing.

What would Private Callahan think of him if he did that?

It was that single thought that pained him the most. If he did as told and sabotaged the investigation, he knew she wouldn't just disapprove, she'd hate him for it. The woman he admired truly believed in the squad and what they were working for; at least, that was the impression he had of her. He respected that about her too; her devotion to their work here. Even though they hadn't spoken, the way she carried herself showed just how seriously she took her job.

And if Thomas followed his alpha's orders, he'd betray that. He'd betray her.

CHAPTER THREE

Jill stood by with her hands folded while Major Williams briefed the squad.

Of course, she paid close attention to the major's words, but that wasn't all she did. She also observed all the team members one by one.

"Firstly, I'd like to welcome our newest team member, Sean McMillan, who we already had the pleasure of working with during the Sevenoaks murder case…"

McMillan should have been the most awkward of the lot; he was new after all. But the tall former police detective seemed completely at ease. He'd even had a twinkle in his eye when he'd greeted everyone as soon as he arrived. Now that his name was being mentioned, he practically beamed with confidence.

Jill scanned the rest of the group. The others were their usual self for the most part.

"I'm sure we will continue to work well together as part of the same squad," the major continued. "But we're still some ways away from that, because as we all know, training comes first. He will undergo boot camp training just like everyone else has. I would like to appoint Bentley as his training officer. In fact, I foresee that Alpha Squad is going to keep growing regularly from now on and I'll need Bentley's help to manage recruitment and training matters."

Jill let her gaze linger on him for a moment. The former Special Forces man had been sour ever since Eric King had been made second-in-command months ago. But even now that the major had singled him out for a promotion, Bentley's firm expression hardly changed. He only acknowledged the announcement with the subtlest twitch in the corner of his mouth.

Jill diverted her attention to the next team member. Cooper was much more easygoing than Bentley, but he'd really come into his own over the last few months. But now, he kept glancing at the new recruit instead of paying attention to the major, perhaps in an attempt to make contact. His behavior seemed to fit with his usual antics, so Jill skipped past him.

"My next announcement relates to a new mission. Secretary Teese's office has received word of a case that could benefit from our special talents, so we will deploy to Blackpool, where the locals have reported a crime spree with potential shifter involvement."

The King brothers stood side-by-side, with Eric fixating on the major and Adam shifting his weight restlessly, as though he couldn't wait for the briefing to be over. Did he have somewhere more interesting to be?

The one person who was behaving completely out of character was also the one Jill normally couldn't stand to look at for more than a second at a time. Thomas

Blackwood's expression was a far cry from his usual cheerful self. He might as well have seen a ghost on the way to the briefing. And it wasn't just that, his entire body language had changed too. Something was definitely wrong, but Jill was in no position to figure out what.

Usually, she did her best to ignore the wolf shifter. That was how uncomfortable his presence made her. But right this moment, she was completely torn and unsure of what to do. A little voice inside her head kept insisting she should work out what was bothering the man so that she might help. At the same time, the more rational part of her brain kept telling her to stay well away from him if she valued her sanity. *What to do?*

"Eric King will be in charge on the mission while I stay on base. Blackwood will have a big role to play, since there have been some wolf sightings around town at the same time that the crimes—petty thefts and burglaries so far— took place. We will need his expertise to bring the case to a satisfactory close."

Jill frowned. Was that why he was acting so strangely? Nerves about taking on more responsibility during the upcoming mission, perhaps?

"Private Callahan will join Eric King and Blackwood on the mission for any logistical support. Adam King and Cooper will accompany them as well. Pack up your things, you leave at 1400 hours."

Jill glanced over at Adam King, and found that he'd stopped fidgeting at last, as though the final announcement had put his mind at ease.

So this was it. The five of them would travel to Blackpool to investigate these burglaries.

Jill took a deep breath and glanced at Thomas Blackwood again. He was still white as a sheet and visibly tense. What on earth had gotten into him this morning?

The major dismissed everyone and the various squad members started chatting to Sean McMillan on their way back inside.

"Funny. I've heard of cat burglars before, not wolf burglars," Cooper quipped.

Bentley scoffed.

"Don't mind old Bentley. He only *acts* tough." Cooper grinned widely, while his remarks earned him a nasty look from the newly appointed training officer of Alpha Squad.

Jill shook her head. No matter how far they'd come, Cooper still had been unable to completely shake his authority issues.

She scanned the group as they entered the barracks and made their way through the narrow hallway. Everyone was right there, chatting excitedly as they usually did before a mission, save for Bentley, of course, whose vocabulary did not seem to include the term 'excitement.'

There was another notable absence. Thomas Blackwood must have slipped away on his own, because he was nowhere to be seen now.

Jill couldn't explain it, but she couldn't shake the

nagging feeling that something was wrong with the man. And more than that, she couldn't understand why she had this growing urge to do something about it. She felt responsible for the smooth running and well-being of the entire squad, sure, but why should it be her job to sort out squad members' personal issues too? It made no sense.

And yet, all the rationalizing in the world couldn't change how she felt.

It was almost as though she could *feel* his unease somehow, as if it had affected her own emotional state and caused her to empathize with him. That made even less sense.

Jill took a deep breath and kept her head down as she marched straight to her office, leaving the rest of the squad to catch up with McMillan on their way to their quarters.

Focus, woman! She chided herself, as she attempted to organize the pending paperwork on her desk. The major's announcement had been clear. Within a few hours, they'd move out to Blackpool, so she only had limited time to finish her work here and pack.

I wonder what Blackwood is up to right now...

Sheesh , her subconscious really wasn't going to let this go.

Jill sunk into her chair and pinched the bridge of her nose. If only her head would stop aching; that ought to help her focus.

She checked her calendar to reminder herself of all pending tasks, when she spotted a familiar date in the not too distant future.

Crap. Jill had been so focused on her work here that she'd forgotten all about her own birthday!

She rummaged around in her desk and located her mobile phone. Lauren wouldn't forgive her if she canceled this year. Ever since their parents passed away, they'd started celebrating their birthday together without fail. It didn't matter how different they were, and how their lives had taken seemingly opposing paths, they were still sisters. Twins, even.

Jill remained still in her chair for a moment, and just stared at the blank screen of her phone. Sure, she was meant to accompany the squad on their newest mission, but they wouldn't miss her that one Sunday, would they? And she'd be in the area anyway, so it wouldn't take too long to drive down to Lauren's place for a bit, then return to the squad by nightfall.

She took a deep breath.

Perhaps a day away from Alpha Squad, and especially Blackwood, would do her good. Give her some distance, some perspective.

She'd have discuss it with the major.

After six months of working flat out without a single day off, surely she'd be open to Jill's request… *Right?*

She collected all her most urgent, pending work, stuffed it in a folder, and headed out to see the major in her office. After knocking twice, she entered, only to find that the major was not alone.

Eric King was with her, and the two of them looked absolutely guilty.

Not that there was a hair out of place on the major, or any other evidence of inappropriate behavior. But they still seemed... flustered.

"I'm sorry," Jill whispered, and started to retreat, reaching for the door so she could close it behind her, when Major Williams stopped her. "I didn't mean to interrupt."

"Wait."

Jill did as she was told, and kept her gaze fixed on the floor in front of her.

"Yes, Ma'am."

"What do you need? Is it about the mission?" the major asked, brushing a non-existent lock of hair out of her face.

She'd put on a stern face, but Jill could tell that she was not entirely comfortable with the situation. Not that it was any of her business, though.

"Actually, well..." *Now or never!* Jill cleared her throat. "I just wanted to let you know I'm ready to go, and also, if it's not too much of an inconvenience, I was hoping to get the second off."

The major paused for a moment, as though she had to think about it.

"That's next Sunday, isn't it? You'll probably still be in Blackpool by then," she said.

Jill nodded. "Yes, Ma'am. Actually, the thing is, it's my

birthday—my sister's also—we're twins. We always spend the day together. If it's a problem, I'll cancel."

Jill waited with bated breath for an answer.

The major glanced over at Eric, who met her gaze. Jill didn't know how she knew, but it seemed like the two of them were talking to each other. Just with looks. It was the strangest thing to observe.

"Sure, no problem, Private. Happy birthday in advance," the major said.

Jill breathed a sigh of relief. She'd never been good at asking for stuff like this for herself. The only reason she'd mustered the courage was because Lauren would eat her alive if she missed it. "Thank you, Ma'am."

"You're dismissed," the major added, not that Jill needed the reminder. She was out the door in a flash, mumbling another thank you.

Awkward .

It was lucky for everyone involved that she hadn't walked in on the two of them in a more compromising position. The resulting conversation about keeping whatever she might have seen to herself was one she was glad to avoid.

Or postpone.

Because it didn't seem like the major and Eric King's relationship was one either of them were planning to cut short. The way they looked at each other spoke volumes.

Will I ever have someone like that?

Jill tried her best to stop thinking about it. In a way, maybe, she almost did. But there was no way she was going to let Thomas Blackwood get close enough to her to find out if he felt the same.

At least she'd managed to get her birthday off, despite everything. She was going to take it as a win and try to focus fully on packing up her stuff before it was time to drive north to Blackpool with most of the squad.

CHAPTER FOUR

The whole afternoon had passed in a blur. Before he knew it, Thomas found himself in yet another police station, in yet another English town, being briefed by cops with attitude problems.

They'd completed a few similar missions, the most difficult of which was the murder case in Sevenoaks some months prior, so none of this was new to any of them. What *was* new was Thomas's mindset. He was used to being the optimistic one; ready to go with the flow, trusting that they would figure things out along the way and come out on top.

Only today his orders were to engineer the exact opposite. Alpha Blackwood had been clear. He was to shut down the investigation somehow.

And all these suspicious cops weren't helping matters. He felt like they could see he had an ulterior motive. That they could look right into the deepest, darkest corners of his mind and identify him as a traitor.

Sweat collected on his brow, and his pulse quickened. Not just that, his entire body tensed up. If he wasn't careful, he'd accidentally shift and attract even more attention to himself.

Deep breaths. You're no good to anyone like this.

He tried to focus on acting normal and finally listen to

the briefing, just like any normal Alpha Squad member would do at a time like this.

"So, interestingly, members of the public have gone on record about seeing a large dog, or a wolf-like creature, in and around the scene of the crime shortly after the break-ins were reportedly committed. This happened at the most recent site as well, a jewelry shop on Church Street," the man in charge of the investigation, who had introduced himself as Detective Tate earlier, said. "We believe that this is how the thieves managed to slip away without getting caught by CCTV."

That didn't help. Thomas tensed up even further.

It was as though he could feel so many pairs of eyes on him, judging him.

He avoided looking at any of the cops, and instead turned slightly, only to find someone else staring at him.

Private Callahan glanced away the moment Thomas looked at her, but that didn't fool him. He'd caught her. She'd been looking in his direction.

Why?

She never looked at him. Actually, for the better part of six months, it was as though she always looked everywhere *but* at him. Much to his frustration.

Ordinarily, he'd be pleased and see this as a sign of a shifting tide in their relationship, but not today. Obviously, she'd picked up on the change in him as well. He was well and truly busted.

The detective stopped speaking, and a whisper passed

through the crowd.

"If you'll excuse me for a moment," Thomas muttered. "Where's your bathroom?"

One of the uniformed policemen who stood off to the side pointed at a door at the far corner of the station.

Thomas breathed a sigh of relief as he fled right through said door. As he stood there in front of the large mirror, splashing water on his face, he couldn't wrap his head around how he was meant to follow his orders.

This investigation was much bigger than just Alpha Squad. Of course it was. They only got called in as a last resort, once the Ministry for Shifter Affairs caught wind of a case that might fall under their purview. But whatever the squad uncovered here, the local police wouldn't just give up.

It was obvious from the way Detective Tate had presented the facts that he took the situation very seriously. He wouldn't just stand back and let Alpha Squad ruin his case.

Thomas had gotten himself into an impossible situation.

He tried to control his heart rate by breathing slowly and deeply in and out. If he didn't stay calm, he'd have even bigger problems. The urge to shift and flee was growing stronger by the second.

And what had gotten into Private Callahan all of a sudden? What a time she'd picked to start paying attention to him.

He forced himself into action and left the restroom to rejoin the squad. Eric King had taken over the briefing and was delegating tasks between the squad and the local police, much to Tate's chagrin.

Cooper was the only one who acknowledged him when Thomas rejoined the group. Thomas forced a smile in an attempt to seem less suspicious.

"Seriously. *Wolf* burglars?" Cooper remarked under his breath.

Looking at the man's silly grin, the remark had probably been an attempt at a joke, but Thomas didn't feel much like laughing. "Right."

"Once your men have identified a list of potential next targets," Eric spoke directly to Tate now. "Then Adam, Thomas and I will stake out some of them at night. We'll have a better chance of keeping our presence unnoticed. We'll get to the bottom of this together."

"We'll see about that," one of the uniformed policemen whispered to another, who chuckled. They'd kept their volume down enough that a human wouldn't have heard the exchange from this far off, but Thomas had picked up on it with complete clarity. No doubt Adam and Eric had heard him too, because the former turned slightly to look at the man who had spoken.

They exchanged a dark look, the meaning of which was crystal clear, without the need for further conversation.

Thomas shrugged and glanced away again. No way was

he going to get into a staring contest with a local cop. Let Adam take the heat, and perhaps he might have a shot at resolving this impossible situation without attracting further suspicion.

Now that the briefing was over, the squad as well as the locals regrouped and discussed their next steps quietly among themselves. If Thomas hadn't received contradictory orders from Rannoch, he would have been completely in support of Eric's plan. It made sense for them to stake out high value targets in the area to intercept the wolves in case they struck again.

Unfortunately, Eric's plan didn't help Thomas. Unless…

If he could intercept the wolves before the rest of the squad got the chance to detain them, perhaps he might be able to warn them… Hopefully, then they'd have enough time to go underground so that neither the local police nor Alpha Squad could arrest them for their crimes.

Alpha Blackwood's orders would be fulfilled, if not literally, then at least in spirit.

"Well, I think this is all we can do for now," Eric spoke up, causing Thomas to flinch slightly. What else had he just said? "Let's head back to the B&B and wait for the detective to send us a list of potential targets. We begin surveillance tonight."

Thomas swallowed hard and nodded in feigned agreement.

"Sure thing," Cooper said. "Perhaps we can take a moment to explore the local area too."

"We're not on holiday here," Eric said.

"No, I know that, but if we're just waiting anyway… I used to come here in the summers when I was little. Family vacations. It would be nice to have a look around is all I'm saying," Cooper pleaded.

"Whatever," Eric said. "But don't take too long. We've got work to do."

"Cheers." Cooper grinned and elbowed Thomas. "Wanna come along? See the tower, the piers, ride a roller coaster at Pleasure Beach? We could all go!"

Thomas blinked a few times, then glanced over at Eric, who stood by with his arms folded and a stern expression on his face.

Adam, meanwhile, tried to stay serious, but a smile soon crept over his face. "I've got a few phone calls to make. You go ahead, mate."

That left Thomas, who enjoyed Cooper's full attention again.

"Uhh, yeah, I think I'll pass, thanks."

"You lot are no fun. Don't you want to relive some good old childhood memories? Where did you go on family holidays when *you* were little?" Cooper demanded.

Thomas shrugged. "We never went on holiday."

Cooper scoffed. "Well, that explains a lot. Fine. I'll go by myself."

What a relief. If everyone was off doing their own thing,

perhaps Thomas would have time to implement his latest plan of warning the local wolves before they got themselves caught. It wasn't perfect, but it was as close to Alpha Blackwood's orders as possible.

There was, of course, one major problem with this plan: how would he track them down first without the support of the rest of the squad? He was a decent enough tracker, but this wasn't anything like the forests back home, where intruders and foreign smells were few and far between.

This was a city with more than 100,000 inhabitants. It wouldn't be easy singling out the people he was after. And before he could even get started, he'd need to get their scent somehow, or else he'd be forced to follow every wolf trail he could find, in the hopes that one of them would lead him to one of the burglars.

The best place to start was, as always, the scene of the most recent crime. During the briefing, he'd overheard Detective Tate say something about a jewelry store, but which one exactly?

As the squad started filtering out of the police station, on their way back to the Land Rover which Private Callahan would drive to the B&B they'd booked, Thomas knew he couldn't just leave without getting that crucial bit of information.

"Say, lads, I have to run back inside for a moment. How about I meet you at the car?" Thomas said, while doing his best to ignore the blatant stare Private Callahan had directed at him.

She was definitely onto him. This was a disaster.

Unfortunately, he didn't have much of a choice.

"I'll be right back," he mumbled, and turned to walk back into the station.

As he passed a few of the cops who had attended the briefing moments earlier, he mumbled something about forgetting his phone, and made his way back into the room where they'd been briefed earlier. On the far wall, there was a large map of the town, with pins marking the locations of the previous break-ins.

Thomas quickly took note of the locations that had been hit most recently, then made it a point to wander out with his phone firmly in his hand. People weren't even paying attention to him anymore, though. Apparently, his excuse had worked.

The rest of the squad was waiting outside, just as expected. He didn't speak a word to any of them on the way to the B&B.

There, he just retreated into his room and waited. It took a while for everyone to settle down.

He listened for activity down the hall, where he knew the others had their rooms. It didn't take long for Cooper to leave; he could tell from the loud, clumsy footsteps that it was him—the only human who had joined their current mission.

Eric and Adam seemed to be safely cooped up inside

with their doors closed; Thomas couldn't hear much noise coming from their positions.

Finally, he did hear a faraway voice: Adam. Possibly he had started making those phone calls he'd mentioned earlier.

Thomas took a deep breath and focused on being as stealthy as possible.

With a bit of luck, nobody would even notice him leaving.

It took but a few minutes for Thomas to make his way down the hall and through the cramped reception area. The girl behind the counter was so enthralled by whatever was playing on the screen of her mobile phone that she didn't bother to look up. That was probably for the best.

Thomas left the B&B in a hurry and headed straight for one of the busier parts of town: Church Street— apparently Blackpool's main shopping destination.

Although the street spanned quite some distance, and he'd failed to note the number of the shop that had recently been broken into, it didn't take him long to locate it. The windows were boarded up, and the door taped up with brightly colored plastic. There was a notice pasted to the door forbidding unauthorized persons from entering the still active crime scene.

Thomas scanned the street. It wasn't safe to enter; there were too many bystanders. Still, he thought he could catch a vaguely familiar scent in the air even outside of the shop.

A wolf had been here recently.

Thomas leaned in closer to the splintered frame that surrounded the door that the burglars had forced open.

There, in between the shattered bits of wood, clung a little tuft of fur.

Thomas's heart sank. Since being sent on this mission, he'd held on at least in part to the belief that the wolf sightings might have been a coincidence. That perhaps the real criminals had started rumors blaming these crimes on the newly outed shifter population in the area. Frame jobs like this weren't too uncommon; the same thing had happened in the Sevenoaks murder case after all.

But the evidence was clear. The sightings seemed to be true.

A shifted wolf had come through here, after the door had been broken down, and left a little bit of himself behind for Thomas to find.

He retrieved a small plastic bag from his pocket and used it to pick up and seal the fur sample. This was it. His first time breaking the law.

He pocketed the evidence and took a deep breath. Orders were orders, though. Illegal or otherwise, he had to follow through and ensure these people did not get themselves caught.

CHAPTER FIVE

Even though the surveillance op was supposed to involve only the shifters on the squad, Jill still tagged along to offer whatever support she could. It was dark, and had been for many hours, so Jill couldn't see very well out of the windscreen of the Land Rover which she had parked around the back from one of the main shopping areas in town. Streetlights were few and far between in this area.

Since the burglars had hit Church Street last, Detective Tate had pointed out a shopping center near the train station as a likely next target. It fit the pattern. The thieves never hit the same area twice in a row, and they'd shown a preference for high end retail stores selling either jewelry or watches. This complex contained many such potential targets.

Still, there was no sign of movement as far as she could tell. The entire area seemed eerily quiet.

So quiet, in fact, that Jill had trouble keeping her eyes open.

Damn sleep deprivation.

Who knows how long she'd been sitting here already, looking at nothing.

The sedate buzzing of the walkie-talkie she had to keep in touch with the rest of the team didn't help. It didn't seem to matter that the interior of the Land Rover was freezing; the cold did nothing to keep her awake.

At last, she drifted off.

As usual during this state of half-sleep she found herself in now, she could only think of one thing. One person, actually.

Thomas Blackwood.

Rushed images of the man passed in front of her mind's eye. His smile, the way the corners of his eyes crinkled slightly when he laughed. He smiled a lot, usually. That was what he was like: kind, cheerful. He was a breath of fresh air in a job that mostly seemed to attract the deadly serious types.

Although Jill wasn't as carefree herself, she could appreciate that in him.

You've got to find out what's wrong with him, an unfamiliar, insistent voice seemed to say.

She looked around. All she could see was white; there was nobody anywhere near. But that didn't matter; it was all just a dream.

"Yes," Jill mumbled. "I must find out."

I mean it. It's important, the voice urged.

"Okay…"

The crackle of the walkie-talkie got louder. Jill looked down and found that she was already holding it. Was that where the strange voice had come from?

Jill pressed the button to speak. "Blackwood. Check in," she said.

Nothing. All she could hear was static.

"Blackwood. Come in please," she repeated.

The walkie-talkie crackled again, but it wasn't Blackwood who answered.

"Callahan, what seems to be the problem?" Eric King asked.

Jill jerked upright, her eyes now wide open as she tried to find her bearings.

The interior of the Land Rover came back into view.

Oh no, I must have dozed off!

Jill waited for her eyes to adjust, but it was too dark out to see much of anything.

"Callahan, come in. Over." Eric King's voice was loud and clear over the walkie-talkie.

Her heart beat faster. How much of what she remembered was a dream, and how much had actually happened?

"Callahan here," she stammered.

"What's going on? Over." Eric asked.

Jill's throat tightened. Damn, had she actually just put a call out to Blackwood in her sleep?

"Never mind, false alarm," she mumbled. "Uhh… Over."

"Please repeat. Over." Eric said.

"I said *never mind*. Forget it." Jill rested her head in her hands. How embarrassing.

"Does anyone have eyes on Blackwood?" Eric asked.

There was a moment of silence before the others

responded.

"Negative," Adam King said.

Callahan looked up through the windscreen, squinting in an attempt to see better in the dark.

There was a strange shadow up ahead, a silhouette on four legs.

No way. Now she was really losing her mind.

She leaned forward, gripping the steering tighter, but whatever she'd just seen—*if* she'd even seen anything at all—had already slipped away into the darkness.

"Blackwood here, what seems to be the problem?"

Relief washed over Jill when she heard his voice. Thank God, he was fine.

"It's early; dawn is only a few hours away. I don't think we'll catch anyone tonight," Eric said. "Retreat. Over."

Jill threw the walkie down onto the passenger seat and rubbed her eyes and patted her cheeks in an attempt to wake up properly. *What the hell had just happened?*

From the weird voice she'd heard in her sleep, to sleep-calling Blackwood with the rest of the team listening in, this was enough excitement for one night.

She was drained, shattered, done. She desperately needed a good night's sleep.

The squad came into view and she turned the key to start the engine.

The old Land Rover coughed a few times before coming to life. It was about time Secretary Teese pulled some strings and got them a better mode of conveyance.

Especially now that McMillan had joined the team; if they ever had to deploy together, they wouldn't all fit into this old rust bucket.

She waited until the three shifters had gotten into the back, then she switched on her lights and carefully navigated the dark, empty streets back to their B&B.

They quietly made their way inside, with Jill entering through the front door last. Just as she closed it behind her, she thought she could hear something. A strange noise, far, far away. It sent shivers down her spine and made the hairs on the back of her neck stand up.

It was like a cry. Or a wolf's howl.

She turned to look at the others, but they were already multiple paces ahead of her and showed no sign of slowing down. They mustn't have heard anything.

Perhaps she'd imagined this as well.

Jill shook her head and checked the door to make sure it was secure. Then she walked straight to her room, only to collapse fully dressed on the bed.

Whatever had happened, she'd analyze it come morning. For now, sleep was her main priority.

———— ◆ ————

Thomas was wired. He should have felt relieved to know that he'd made it back without tipping any of the others off, but he felt anything but calm.

He paced around his cramped little room, back and

forth, until it threatened to make him dizzy.

They'd almost caught him. *Almost.*

When he'd gone out in the afternoon to track down the pack responsible for the break-ins, he hadn't succeeded. Not even close.

Sure, he got the fur sample, and a good whiff of what these people—or at least one of them—smelled like. But he hadn't been able to track them.

Before he'd gotten the chance to follow their trail through the maze that was Blackpool town center, he'd gotten a call from Eric King telling him to report to the B&B for a briefing.

Detective Tate had sent over a list of potential targets, and they had to work out together how to manage the first surveillance op of this mission.

So he was forced to abort his own hunt and return to their temporary base of operations, Eric's room at the B&B.

There they'd formulated a plan for the night which involved the three of them—Eric, Adam and Thomas himself—positioned at strategic locations around a local retail center which contained some potential targets which the burglars might be tempted to hit next.

Meanwhile, Thomas considered his own plan. He had to make sure he'd intercept the burglars himself if they showed up. He had to warn them.

And that was exactly what he'd tried to do.

Thomas rubbed the bruise on his chest, where one of

the burglars had struck him when he'd surprised him in one of the dark alleys around the mall.

What was meant as a friendly warning had not been received as such. At least not at first.

But Thomas had done what he could. As soon as he'd caught the young wolf who was suspiciously hanging around toward the back of one of the jewelry stores on Detective Tate's list, Thomas had let him know Alpha Squad was onto him. And if he knew what was best for him and his accomplices, he would turn around and give up on tonight's hit.

He never got the young man's name. Or any other information that might help him locate the rest of the crew.

The only thing Thomas had gotten out of the entire exercise was a punch in the chest and the resulting damaged pride. If his current orders weren't to keep these idiots safe, he would have taught the kid a lesson he would never forget.

What was up with this local pack, anyway? The kid he caught couldn't have been older than nineteen or twenty. If Thomas had gotten into this kind of a mess during his younger years, he would have been punished dearly for it.

He'd discuss it with Alpha Blackwood. There was no setup or conspiracy. These were a bunch of wolves up to no good. The alpha would disapprove for sure; he had to. This kind of behavior was inexcusable where Thomas came from. Why should Blackpool wolves live by different rules than the rest of his kind?

Thomas checked the alarm clock on the bedside table. It was just before six in the morning. The alpha was an early riser. Chances were that he'd already be up.

Thomas dialed the number and waited. As usual, his aunt Rebecca picked up.

"Hello?" she asked.

"Thomas, here. I hope I didn't wake you."

"Oh, not at all. I've been up for an hour already. How are you doing? Is everything alright?"

Thomas couldn't help but smile. How nice to hear a sympathetic voice, especially now that his mission seemed to be falling apart at the seams.

"Everything is great, Aunt Rebecca. I must speak with the alpha, though."

"Of course. I'll get him."

Thomas waited until Alpha Blackwood's stern voice could be heard on the other end.

"Thomas. Have you been successful?" the alpha asked.

Thomas took a deep breath. "This case—the investigation is a lot bigger than we thought."

"So you've failed?"

"What I mean is, perhaps we need to rethink our strategy... Sir."

The alpha scoffed. "*Strategy.* You've been hanging out with these military types for too long. Son, I told you I don't want this... this *squad* of yours pinning a bunch of crimes on fellow wolves. I thought I'd made myself clear."

"The thing is, it isn't a lie or a false accusation. There really is a pack of young wolves in Blackpool who are robbing local shops after closing. I caught one of them tonight."

"You *what*? I told you I don't want anyone finding out about this or getting the wrong idea, and you've gone and *caught* one? How in the world does that come even close to following my orders? Or am I to assume that you're making a play for alpha yourself. Is that it?"

Thomas shook his head. He really wasn't taking this very well.

"Not at all, Sir. I mean I warned the young man. I warned him to stay away if he didn't want to get caught. Nobody else on the squad even saw him. I also collected some evidence, a fur sample that was left behind at the scene of a previous break-in. I've kept it safe. Nobody will find it."

The alpha sighed deeply on the other end.

"Very well. I can see that you're at least *trying* to do the right thing. Clumsily or otherwise."

"Sir, the thing I can't seem to understand is, are we meant to let these crimes go unpunished? Is that what our kind is reduced to now, common thefts and break-ins?"

"Thomas, you'll listen to me very carefully. These are *your orders*. Don't think too much beyond what I'm about to tell you."

"Yes, Sir," Thomas mumbled.

"You will find the leader of the pack and have a quiet word with him. These wolves are to leave town, at least until the dust settles. Once the investigation is closed for lack of evidence—as I trust it will be thanks to your intervention—we can all go back to our normal lives."

Thomas frowned. So he was planning on letting them get away with everything. What a hypocrite!

He immediately caught himself and tried to swallow his frustration. He shouldn't indulge in such criticisms and insults. Not against his own alpha. It went against everything he was raised to believe in.

Then again, so did a pack of wolves choosing a life of crime.

Thomas shook his head and took a deep breath.

"Yes, Alpha. I will convey the message. Once the pack leaves town and the investigation dies down, we can all go back to the way things were."

"Good. I'm counting on you, son!"

Thomas cringed slightly when the alpha called him *son*.

"Yes, Sir." Thomas nodded to make his point, even though obviously Alpha Blackwood couldn't see it through the phone. Then he hung up.

What a mess.

Even if the alpha and he didn't see eye-to-eye on this, Thomas had tried to do the right thing. That was all he could do, right? Now he had new orders to follow, whether he liked it or not.

CHAPTER SIX

Thomas had slept on everything, however briefly, and still he couldn't quite understand why Alpha Blackwood would endorse such criminal behavior. These wolves were giving their fellow shifters a bad name.

Perhaps that was what he was worried about; if it all came out, it would no doubt garner a lot of media attention. Victor Domnall and his followers would use it as ammunition to continue the smear campaign they'd started against shifters months ago, when they'd tried to pin the Sevenoaks murders on the shifter refugees that lived in the area.

That was the only justification Thomas could come up with, anyway. For now, it had to suffice.

He was dressed and ready by eight, along with the rest of the squad. Adam, Cooper, and himself waited in the lobby of the B&B. Their leader, Eric, was the last to join them.

The two bear shifters looked a bit worse for wear, making Cooper the only squad member who seemed fresh as a daisy this morning.

But the short and restless night they'd had didn't bother Thomas directly. He had bigger problems.

How would he track down the rest of the criminal crew without anyone else on the squad noticing?

Eric King cleared his throat before addressing the squad.

"Our surveillance op last night did not bear fruit, unfortunately. But the plan is still sound. We'll keep staking out prime locations in town every night until the burglars inevitably show themselves again."

Oh, great. More sleepless nights.

From the corner of his eye, Thomas noticed that Private Callahan had joined the squad. She looked tired as well, which wasn't surprising considering she'd joined them on the night shift.

Her presence distracted, as usual. Thomas found himself glancing in her direction again and again. He wasn't quite sure what he was hoping for. Having her stare at him yesterday at the police station had been unnerving as well as exciting in a way.

The frustrating thing was that he could not read her properly. He couldn't make out if she was looking at him more often now because she was suspicious of what he was up to, or if that was just his own paranoia talking.

He forced himself to direct his full attention at Eric again. With so many things on his plate, he couldn't afford the additional distraction.

No matter how enticing.

"While it's still light out, we'll go through the evidence the local police have collected at the various sites of the burglaries, as well as study surveillance footage of the area. Perhaps we'll find something that's so far been overlooked."

This didn't sound promising. If they were all together studying evidence, how would Thomas slip away unnoticed?

He raised his hand.

"Yes, Blackwood?" Eric said.

"Umm, how about I canvass the local wolf population as well. Figure out if they've heard anything," Thomas suggested. It was the best he could come up with.

"Great idea, we can split up and—"

Thomas shook his head. No, that wouldn't work for him.

"I really think it's best if I handle it. Wolves can be suspicious of outsiders. They'll be more likely to open up to me as I'm one of their own," he explained.

Eric folded his arms and kept his eyes fixed on Thomas's face as he seemed to consider his request. That was enough to make his nerves flare up again. Would he look right through his excuse?

"Isn't that what the major wanted? For me to take on some extra responsibilities on this case?" Thomas added.

Eric finally nodded, much to Thomas's relief.

"Very well. You make an excellent point. Blackwood will liaise with the local wolf population while the rest of us spend time looking over the collected evidence. Questions?"

Thomas glanced left, at Adam, then right at Cooper

and Callahan. Nobody stirred.

Thank God.

He might just get away with it after all.

------◆------

Armed with the fur sample from the most recent break-in site, as well as the knowledge of what his assailant from last night smelled like, Thomas didn't take long to find a trail. He'd started at the mall where he'd had his run-in with the young wolf and followed his scent from there. Soon, the youngster's scent had mixed and mingled with other wolf trails, and most of them seemed to be converging in one direction.

It was a bit of a walk, straight across town, until Thomas found himself in an industrial area set along the railway line.

But his destination wasn't among the large warehouses and busy parking lots surrounding them. Thomas tracked the scent all the way to a railway crossing that led to a wooded area which the casual observer might assume was unpopulated. Set just between a quiet residential road and the train tracks, this patch of dense vegetation seemed to be home to mostly birds and small animals, as well as the odd drifter looking for a quiet place to rest.

But Thomas knew better. This was where his nose had led him.

This small woodland belonged to the wolves he'd been

tracking. He'd entered their domain.

"Well, what do we have here?" someone asked.

"That's the guy I told you about," another, younger voice whispered. Thomas recognized it as belonging to the young wolf he'd gotten into a confrontation with the other night.

He turned around and studied the shrubbery, but he couldn't see anything or anyone. But that didn't mean there was nobody there. They were watching him and they were very close; he could smell as well as hear them.

"I'm Thomas Blackwood," he introduced himself. "Nephew to the Alpha of the Blackwood clan in Rannoch, Scotland."

The two voices mumbled something amongst themselves; Thomas couldn't make out what was being said.

"So?" the more authoritative of the two said. "This is our land. You're trespassing."

Thomas snorted. "Trespassing? Yeah, about that. You've been robbing local businesses. And you're drawing an awful lot of attention to yourselves. Be glad I'm the one who's trespassing and not the police. Or worse."

"We're only taking our fair share. The humans always looked down on us. They used to call us pikeys. Now they've got loads-a new names to choose from. Shifter scum. Mutt."

Thomas rolled his eyes. *Oh, the tragedy.* He'd heard of

packs like these. Drifters. Travelers.

Rather than make a home somewhere in the many forestlands that still existed further north, they chose to live near humans, while making no effort whatsoever to integrate into society. No wonder people were suspicious of them. If his time with Alpha Squad had taught him one thing, it was that segregation was the root of many evils.

And worse, those suspicions weren't unfounded in this particular case. They really *were* criminals.

Unfortunately, he still had his orders.

"Look, we're of the same blood. I'm not here to argue with you or intrude into your territory. But it's only a matter of time before you get yourselves caught. I'm here to prevent that from happening."

The leaves rustled, and a man appeared.

Broad shoulders, reddish-blond hair, and steely blue eyes. The weathered and deep tan skin on his face suggested he'd spent most of his life outdoors. It was near impossible to guess his age for the same reason.

"Thomas Blackwood," Thomas introduced himself again and stretched out his hand.

The man didn't move. Thomas shrugged and pulled his hand back again.

"Why should I believe you're here to help us?" the man asked finally.

Thomas retrieved the small sealed bag with the fur he'd found yesterday and held it up in front of him. "You or one of your boys left something behind when you hit that jewelry shop the other night."

The man reached out for the bag, but Thomas pulled back just in time. "Not so fast. I've introduced myself. Now I'd love to know who I'm negotiating with."

The man raised an eyebrow and folded his arms. Clearly, he wasn't nearly as impressed as Thomas would have liked.

"And you're from Rannoch, you say?"

Thomas nodded.

"Is Eric Blackwood still alpha or has someone taken his place?"

Thomas paused. The man knew a lot more about Thomas's home than he'd initially let on.

"Yes, he's my uncle."

The man nodded. "Okay, follow me."

Thomas did as told, and as they walked along a narrow pathway through the shrubs, they soon found themselves in front of a collection of caravans.

Outside the first one stood the young wolf who'd punched him in the chest during their first meeting.

Thomas eyed him suspiciously, while the youngster stared back.

A young woman sat outside one of the caravans with a baby in her lap. As soon as she spotted Thomas, she got up and hurried inside, closing the door behind her.

Slowly, a couple more young men appeared in the clearing and formed a circle around Thomas.

That made half a dozen to one. It was difficult—no, impossible—not to feel at least a little threatened.

"So. You've taken it upon yourself to warn us that the police is coming for us?" the man with the reddish hair asked. A quick look around revealed he was the most senior wolf of the group. He had to be their alpha.

Thomas averted his gaze. He did it out of habit mostly, though it was also the respectful thing to do.

"Well I wouldn't say I've taken it upon myself… I have orders from Alpha Blackwood to ensure you don't get caught."

"And why would he send you on such a mission? All the way from Rannoch?" the man asked.

"I wasn't in Rannoch," Thomas said. He thought for a moment. Did these people even follow the news?

"I'm a member of Alpha Squad. Perhaps you've heard of it?" Thomas asked finally.

"Alpha Squad. That name sounds vaguely familiar."

"It's a task force set up by the government to help with shifter related matters. My team mates and I have been sent in to investigate these burglaries."

"So the police aren't actually after us, *you* are?" The man took a step forward, as did all his underlings.

Thomas raised both his hands in what he hoped would be seen as a calming gesture.

"Technically, but I report to my alpha. It is on his orders that I joined Alpha Squad in the first place," Thomas said. It was awkward, having to admit everything aloud.

"Continue." The man took a step back again, and his pack seemed to relax a bit too.

"Anyway, I have orders not to let you get caught. My alpha advises you to leave town, at least until all of this blows over, only to return when the coast is clear."

The man paced back and forth a few times, before stopping and addressing Thomas again.

"And this evidence you found. Nobody else knows about it?"

Thomas shook his head while resting his hand protectively on the bag that was once again safely in his pocket.

"I suppose we could leave for a wee bit. Let things die down. But one question remains."

"What's that?" Thomas asked.

"What does Eric Blackwood, Alpha of Rannoch, want in return? What's in it for him?"

Thomas pressed his lips together. That was the one question he had no answer to. As much as he'd tried to ignore it and just blindly follow his orders, it did bother him that he had no idea.

What *was* in it for Alpha Blackwood?

"I'm afraid I can't answer that," Thomas said. "You'll have to ask him yourself when you get the chance."

The man smiled briefly, then turned away. "Well, I thank you for your visit. We will do as you suggest and lay low for a while. It's too bad, because we had our eye on quite a sweet little haul, which would've gone a long way toward feeding us this summer."

Perhaps getting every one of these strapping young lads a job would help with that. Thomas kept this remark to himself.

"I better join my squad, before they wonder where I've run off to," Thomas said.

The man nodded. "You do that, Thomas Blackwood from Rannoch."

Thomas turned away and found the young wolf he'd met earlier staring at him. All the frustration and anger he felt about this assignment bubbled back up to the surface. He couldn't leave without at least getting a little something off his chest.

"One thing," Thomas said.

"Yes?"

"You might want to teach this young lad here how to behave around his seniors. Punching first and asking questions later is frowned upon in polite company."

The young lad bared his teeth, but held his ground. Clearly, he wasn't in agreement with Thomas's assessment.

The pack's alpha—name as yet unknown—chuckled. "We'll bear that in mind for when we find ourselves in polite company, won't we, boys?"

Thomas swallowed his anger and marched back along the path he'd entered from, through the shrubs and back onto the narrow road that crossed the railway line, without looking back even once.

It was done. Hopefully now he could wash his hands of the whole wretched story. He couldn't wait for things to get back to normal.

CHAPTER SEVEN

All day, Jill had been with Eric, Adam, and Cooper, driving them back and forth between the police station and various crime scenes. She wasn't sure if it was all in her head, but she couldn't shake the nagging feeling that something was about to go very wrong.

Blackwood had gone off by himself to talk to the local wolf population in an effort to gain intelligence from them, which was both a blessing and a curse.

The weird incident that happened the previous night, where she'd radioed him in her sleep, still played on her mind. Jill still had no idea why she would do a thing like that. All she could remember was that somehow she'd felt he was in danger and that feeling remained had with her throughout the day.

Perhaps it was the stresses of the job. That had to be it. Stress could do funny things to a person.

But the memory of the voice that had spoken to her in her dream was still crystal clear. It had instructed her to find out what was going on with Blackwood, and no matter how hard she tried, she couldn't ignore it forever.

So when they returned to the B&B for some much needed rest before the upcoming second night of surveillance, Jill was relieved to find that Blackwood was already there.

But old habits were hard to shake. She kept her distance from the man, taking a seat all the way across the B&B's common room from him, and just observed as Eric King asked for a report on Blackwood's findings.

"Have you discovered anything that could help the case?" Eric asked.

Blackwood seemed reluctant to answer. Or was Jill imagining things again?

"Not really. I spoke to a few families in the area, and they seemed to have no idea about these crimes. Perhaps the culprits aren't locals," Blackwood said.

Jill couldn't pretend she knew him well enough to be able to tell when he was lying, but… Well, it did seem like he wasn't being entirely truthful. The way he leaned back from Eric just slightly, subconsciously trying to put distance between himself and his squad leader, was unusual for him. Blackwood seemed to make extra effort to maintain eye contact, which looked forced.

Eric, meanwhile, acted completely normal. Like he hadn't picked up on the little cues Jill thought she could see.

While Eric and Blackwood continued their discussion, Jill tried to focus on her own job for the evening. Just because they were out on a mission didn't mean she didn't have to keep up with shifter related news anymore.

Jill picked up her bag and retrieved her private iPad. She'd subscribed to various news outlets on it, perfect for situations such as these when she was out of the office.

Flipping through article after article, everything seemed to be much of the same old. Until…

There, labeled as regional news on BBC Scotland, was a little article that immediately attracted her attention.

"Local wolf shifter joins SNP in Perth & Kinross Council bid"

Jill sat back in her chair and waited for the article to load. This was unheard of. Sure, the New Alliance had been active on social media and had done numerous TV appearances since its inception, but their focus had been education, not political influence. For a shifter to step into public view was no small decision; most were very private people. How could they not be? For centuries, they'd made it their life's mission to stay in the shadows…

The article went on to explain that this wolf shifter who had joined the Scottish National Party had actually managed to get their support to stand in the local elections in one of the Scottish councils. Jill read on and felt her heart beating just a little bit faster.

The man was from Rannoch; that was where Blackwood was from.

She glanced up only to find that Blackwood was now sitting by himself again, quietly sipping a cup of tea.

Jill continued to read the article and paused on something else. The candidate's name: Eric Blackwood.

How many Blackwoods hailed from Rannoch? This couldn't be a coincidence. They must know each other, perhaps even be related.

Jill closed the page and put the iPad down on the table beside her.

This was significant, something she ought to look into. Perhaps she should just ask him about it? That would certainly be easiest. If only she knew how to start that conversation without making things awkward between them…

Blackwood looked up and their eyes met. Jill felt her throat close up and her heart tried to hammer its way out of her chest.

She wasn't super confident, but she'd never known herself to be *this* nervous about anything, or anyone.

It was all a test, she concluded. This entire deal with the other wolf named Blackwood standing in local elections. It was divine or cosmic intervention for her to face her fears.

Jill pushed her chair back and got up, reluctantly.

Now or never.

She walked over to Blackwood, who continued to stare at her. Was she reading into things too much or were his eyes just a little bit too wide for comfort? Was *he* nervous too? *Preposterous.*

"Uhh, hi," Jill said. "I was wondering if I could have a word."

Blackwood frowned and looked around, as though there was any doubt Jill was really speaking directly to him.

"Sure… what do you want to discuss?" he asked after a

short, awkward pause.

She took a deep breath and averted her gaze. It was simply too uncomfortable to continue to make eye contact with the man. Infuriating, how weak he made her feel.

"I think we should talk about it in private," she spoke in a low whisper.

Oh God, that sounded totally wrong, didn't it? Too bad she'd realized it too late.

Thomas muttered something she couldn't understand and got up in a rush, almost knocking his chair over in the process. He caught it, though.

Such fast reflexes.

Jill held her breath as she waited for him, then started walking in the direction of the hallway leading to their rooms. *Somewhere private. Good God, was she actually taking him to her room? That would be completely inappropriate!*

"Here will be fine," Jill said, after making sure there was nobody else in the vicinity.

"Okay…" Thomas turned to face her.

Oh my, those deep blue eyes. This was the closest she'd ever been to him both literally and figuratively, and for good reason. Now that she was alone with him, in the relative privacy of this empty hallway, she found it hard to remember what she wanted to talk about.

"You…" Jill started, then closed her eyes in order to refocus.

"Yes?" Thomas asked.

His voice was so warm and smooth, like hot chocolate.

That doesn't even make any sense, a voice like hot chocolate, Jill corrected herself.

"Are you related to Eric Blackwood?" she asked, and opened her eyes again to gauge his reaction.

He pulled back and frowned. "Yes, he's my uncle. Why do you ask?"

Jill shrugged. Her mind was blank.

Now that they were both here, it didn't seem important anymore.

His scent overwhelmed her. Like a fine cologne, she was certain she'd remember it forever, even if she never saw him again. The attraction she felt toward him was too much to bear.

"I want to know you," Jill blurted out, then covered her mouth with her hand. Damn, why had she said *that?*

Thomas smiled. "Me too. Though I feel like somehow I already know you quite well."

His smile was contagious. She returned it. That was how she felt. Like they were already connected somehow.

"Then maybe we need to go inside." Jill gestured at his room, up the hall. "Before someone intrudes."

In the process of pulling her hand back, it brushed past his. Or had he brushed past hers? It didn't matter.

Something came over her. A madness, a fever which she couldn't control.

The little voice of reason inside her head tried to kick and scream, but Jill didn't really care anymore. It went against everything she believed in, getting this close to a squad member. And yet it felt so… right?

She slipped her hand into the crook of Blackwood's arm, and her knees threatened to buckle underneath her. Luckily, it wasn't much of a walk.

By the time they'd reached Blackwood's room, Jill's defenses were way down. One could say that they were non-existent.

In a few days' time, she'd turn thirty. The big three-oh. And never before in her life had she felt the way she did right now, clinging to the broad, muscular arm of a man she should stay the hell away from.

But she couldn't.

She could no longer resist the pull she felt toward him. From the moment she'd allowed herself to finally get close to him, the floodgates seemed to have been opened. Like this was meant to happen all along, and she'd been stupid to fight it.

And now, *God*, she didn't even know what she was doing or where it would lead.

There was no analyzing it, no stopping it. Sure, she had a pretty good idea where their instincts and urges might get them physically. But what did it *mean?*

He cupped her face and gazed longingly into her eyes.

This . This was what every girl in the whole world wanted. To be seen as he saw her. To be cherished and admired.

"You're beautiful," he whispered.

The rawness in his voice made her knees weak again. It was like a dream.

She wanted to respond, but she couldn't find the words.

Instead, she tiptoed toward him as he leaned down further, allowing their lips to touch. If the way he'd looked at her just now was the most glorious experience of her life so far, this was a million times better.

Her heart skipped a few beats. The softness of his lips, the tenderness of his touch. Everything about him was beautiful. His kisses promised a surprising gentleness along with a searing passion Jill had never found in another lover.

Like they were made for one another.

She could be shy, nervous even. But with the right man… There was a whirlwind of emotions hidden beneath the surface, yet to be uncovered.

As their tongues touched just slightly, darting around each other in a dance of discovery and wonder, everything changed yet again. Something else happened that Jill had never experienced before.

It was as though she was no longer alone in her head.

Sure, she still had that critical voice telling her to stop what she was doing and run, but it was getting weaker. There was *another* presence in her mind also. Thomas Blackwood.

Wolf. Warrior. Lover.

Jill opened her eyes and gazed deeply into his. So much to see.

When she wrapped her arms around him and kissed him again, a flood of images entered her mind. His thoughts and emotions.

His memories.

There were glimpses of how he'd watched her. On base as well as on previous missions. He'd been pining for her as she had done for him.

She also saw visions of his home town. Moors and forests that spanned as far as the eye could see.

But along with all these beautiful memories, there was something darker lurking underneath it all. Conversations with his uncle, Eric Blackwood. Secret outings that did not fit into Alpha Squad's mission.

Jill pulled back, her heart beating frantically now, not due to the increasing passion she'd felt for him—though the attraction was even stronger now. No, this was something else. Fear. Hurt.

Betrayal.

"You've been sabotaging the case," Jill stammered.

Thomas took a step back, his face suddenly white as a sheet.

"I… I had orders."

Jill's eyes burned with the onset of tears. Her biggest fear about getting too close to Thomas Blackwood had been related to her professional integrity. This was so, so much worse.

"So do I. We all have orders," she whispered. "The difference is who we take them from."

"You don't understand..." Thomas argued. His voice sounded as deflated as he looked.

Everything fell into place. This was what he had been so torn up about since Alpha Squad had landed this mission.

Jill shook her head. She didn't want to hear it. After the earlier high she'd felt with him, this sudden crash was unbearable.

"You can't play for two teams. Everyone must choose eventually." Her voice was choked and her vision blurry.

The headaches she'd suffered for weeks now were back with a vengeance.

"I believe in the squad. In what we're doing here," Thomas stammered.

"No. You've made your choice already."

"I'll make it up to you. I'll—"

Jill raised her hand and glared at him through wet eyelashes. "You'll leave. Promise me you'll leave."

Thomas pressed his lips together. She could barely look at him anymore.

I can't turn you in. I don't know why, but I just can't. Don't make me, Jill thought.

Thomas took a step forward, but she flinched away.

I understand, his voice entered her mind.

Jill wanted to scream, to force him to sever this

connection between them.

Not that it helped, because he was still there, sharing her mind with her.

I'll go now. Know that I'm sorry.

Promise you won't come back. Promise you won't make me reconsider, Jill thought.

Thomas nodded and picked up his squad issue duffel bag from the chair in the corner of the room, before starting to randomly throw items of clothing into it.

Tears streamed freely down Jill's cheeks. Enough. This had all been a big mistake.

She ran out of the room without saying another word.

CHAPTER EIGHT

Thomas had completely screwed up. This was by far the worst mistake he'd made in his entire life.

He knew this now, when it was too late to take it back.

He'd betrayed the squad, and as a result, betrayed *her*. Jill Callahan. The woman of his dreams.

And she was right to send him away for it. Actually, she should have turned him in; in a way it would have been better if she had.

But she hadn't been able to. It was too painful, perhaps.

After packing up just a few of his belongings and stuffing them into his bag, he'd left the B&B unnoticed. Well, almost unnoticed. Like a homing beacon, he could feel Jill's presence in the same building, and he was certain she could sense him too. Until he stepped outside and the distance between them had grown so much that the magic no longer worked.

Then, he'd just started walking. Aimlessly, endlessly.

He wasn't sure where he was going, and he didn't care.

The world—his alpha and everyone else—could go to hell.

There was nothing here for him anymore.

He instinctively kept going the same direction: east. As far away from Alpha Squad and Jill as he could manage.

For hours and hours, he hiked along brightly lit dual carriageways, small country roads, and even along a motorway. He passed through small towns and villages, only stopping once in the middle of the night at a petrol station for a much needed break.

So the following morning, after a whole night of walking, he found himself in a busy little cafe, the type where tradesmen go to have a hearty full breakfast in the morning.

He wasn't hungry, not really.

But if he was going to make it through the day, he needed the nourishment, so he'd ordered anyway.

By the time his plate arrived, piled high with eggs, two sausages, some bacon, mushrooms, and fried tomatoes, he almost regretted his decision. Not that the food wasn't nice.

His throat had all but closed up. His stomach was growling in protest.

He pushed the plate away and closed his eyes, trying to will the nausea away.

"What's wrong, love?" a raspy female voice asked. "Bad morning? Long night?"

He looked up and found that it was the woman who'd taken his order; she was in her fifties or perhaps even early sixties, her voice raw with what Thomas guessed might be the side effects of a decades-long smoking habit.

"Something like that," he mumbled.

"Why don't you get some coffee in ya, that'll help sort

things out," she suggested, and held up a thermos.

Thomas nodded.

"I see a lot of you young boys in 'ere, believe it or not."

Thomas had no trouble believing that.

"Look like your lives have just ended. Trust me. It ain't the end. There's more fish in the sea and all that."

Thomas blinked a few times, but didn't say anything.

She was trying to cheer him up, which was nice enough. But he wasn't in the mood. And anyway, this lady was a human. She couldn't possibly comprehend the loss he was going through. Wolves didn't just go through partners again and again.

They mated once. For life.

Jill had been his one chance at happiness and companionship—at love—and he'd blown it.

Still, he nodded at the woman, who smiled briefly and turned around to serve some of the other customers.

Thomas held onto the mug of steaming coffee with both hands, almost indifferent to the heat emanating from it as it burned his fingertips. Physical pain could not compare with what he felt inside.

"Mate," another voice interrupted his thoughts.

Thomas turned around and found that it was a balding man in work overalls who sat the adjacent table.

"Don't listen to old Sheila. If your lady's worth it, you gotta fight to keep her. Know what I mean?"

Thomas wasn't quite sure what to make of this place.

These people, one after the other, giving him relationship advice. They didn't even know the first thing about his predicament. Was this normal human behavior? Strange didn't even begin to cover it.

He nodded politely and turned back to face his own table again.

Perhaps he should get out of here, before any of the other patrons decided to join in the conversation.

A TV in the corner attracted his attention. Although the volume was set low, he could just about understand every word if he really focused. It was some news program set in a shiny, modern studio. The female reporter was speaking into the camera about the challenges faced by the current government in managing the integration of the various shifter communities in the country. Ordinarily, the discussion wouldn't have interested Thomas much, if it hadn't been for a familiar name the reporter had taken. Rannoch.

He pulled his plate closer and started chewing on a bit of lukewarm bacon. Although he hated to admit it to himself, the food did help, so he kept eating while watching the TV.

The camera panned to the right and showed someone familiar. Eric Blackwood, Thomas's uncle and the root cause of his current predicament.

"Could you turn that up, please?" Thomas asked and turned around to the woman, Sheila. She frowned, but then did as he had asked.

"So, as Alpha of Rannoch, you are at the forefront of these challenges. What do you think the government should be doing to improve the situation on-ground?" the reporter asked.

"I'm not quite sure what they *can* do. I believe in a proactive leadership style. Lead by example. And during my campaign, I intend to answer all these questions and more and lay out an exact plan for the betterment of shifterkind all over the country."

Campaign? What on earth was he talking about?

Thomas kept listening and eating. Before he knew it, he'd finished the whole breakfast.

"As the first member of the shifter community to run for public office, you are a trailblazer, a pioneer entering unknown territory. I've heard that many members of your own community in Rannoch lead a very insular lifestyle; in short, you don't head out much and keep to yourselves. What has inspired you to take such a giant step into the spotlight?"

Alpha Blackwood smiled and nodded. "Well, I'll be honest; it wasn't my wish for our existence to become common knowledge, at least not at first. But now that we're out, we owe it to ourselves to make the best of it. I just took a look at the political scene and noticed that nobody can really speak for us, not as well as one of our own could."

"That's an excellent point. Thank you very much for

joining us today, Mr. Blackwood. And I do wish you good luck in the upcoming elections."

The news channel's logo filled the screen while a voice-over announced the next feature.

Thomas sat back in his chair and tried to fill in the blanks between what he'd just heard. Alpha Blackwood was running for office? This must have been what Jill had asked about him in the first place; she'd found out about this first. And when she'd figured out what he'd been up to, she'd come to the only logical conclusion: the Alpha's orders had been entirely self-serving. He'd wanted to make sure that the burglaries in Blackpool remained unsolved so that his own political career could take off. Media hype about a wolf pack indulging in criminal behavior would certainly damage his bid. People generally didn't take long to jump to conclusions, not when it came to people who were fundamentally different, like a whole other species.

As a member of the Rannoch pack, this knowledge did not change anything. Orders were still orders, and he still had a duty to follow them to the best of his abilities. Only, it *did* change things. Along with the stab of regret over how things had turned out with Jill, Thomas felt something else he'd never had to face before. Disillusionment. He'd lost faith in his Alpha.

The humans in this place had been nice enough; at least they'd tried to be in their own way. But for the first time since joining Alpha Squad six months ago, he longed to be back home. To roam the forests and moors, to let his wolf run across the wilderness without a soul in sight.

Of course, that was not an option—Alpha Blackwood would be furious that he got himself caught. He'd see that as yet another threat against his budding political ambitions. And Thomas was pretty sure he could no longer look the man in the eye anymore either.

He was just an underling, not a leader. So the Alpha technically did not owe him any explanation about why he wanted Alpha Squad's case to fizzle out. Still, all of this left a bitter taste in Thomas's mouth.

He'd felt it as soon as he realized the wolves in Blackpool had really been behind the crimes they were investigating. The Alpha was wrong in letting them get away with it. Knowing his agenda made things infinitely worse.

Thomas had initially thought that the drifters he'd met were simple folk, but their alpha's question had been the most pertinent yet: in exchange for his help, what did Alpha Blackwood want in return? Maybe this first election was just step one in a bigger plan. Maybe one day he'd come knocking on doors for wider political support.

And when he did, those drifters would be indebted to him, which was clever and a bit disturbing.

Who knew how many such deals a man like Alpha Blackwood would be willing to make? How flexible were his morals if he was happy to let a bunch of thieves walk after it was proved beyond a doubt they were guilty?

No, he couldn't go back to Rannoch, perhaps ever. Neither could he go back to the squad, not after promising Jill he'd leave so she didn't have to turn him in.

But he couldn't just sit around and waste more time feeling sorry for himself either. He had to *do* something. In light of what he'd learned from the news this morning, maybe his own investigation shouldn't yet be over.

Thomas pulled a tenner out of his wallet and left it on the table. Then, he resolutely pushed his chair back and headed straight for the door.

"Your change!" Sheila called after him.

He waved in her direction without turning around. "Keep it."

Sure, Thomas lost everything he'd ever longed for yesterday evening, but that technically hadn't been his own fault. He'd only been following orders. Now, he had to find a way out of this mess, to follow his own destiny and not somebody else's.

For the first time in Thomas's life, he felt free. The shackles of his past no longer controlled him, which was a liberating realization, as well as a terrifying one. He could make his own choices; do what was best, not just for himself but for his people. For his squad, even?

The problem was, he didn't yet know how to make the most of this newfound clarity.

He had to come up with a plan.

CHAPTER NINE

A commotion outside Jill's room prompted her to get up. It was late; the darkness outside the window told her as much, but she wasn't asleep yet anyway. How could she sleep after what happened earlier?

Jill still couldn't reconcile how things had gone so terribly wrong, right after the utter perfection that was their first kiss. She unlocked her door.

"Has anyone seen him?" Eric King demanded.

Jill blinked to let her eyes adjust to the light in the hallway. The incomplete squad came into view. Eric, Adam, Cooper.

Thomas Blackwood was missing, obviously.

"Private Callahan," Eric addressed her, as she awkwardly adjusted the top of her night suit.

"Yes?"

"Have you seen Blackwood?"

She pressed her lips together. It felt wrong to lie to them. But she was covering for herself as much as Thomas, so she shook her head.

"Haven't seen him since around… I want to say, six in the evening?" At least that much was true. Eric would never get the full story from her.

"We were going to go stake out the local area again, but he never reported for duty," Adam explained.

Well, at least he'd done as promised and left. Of course Jill already knew this. Their first kiss had caused some kind of connection or link to form between them. Not a figurative connection, but an actual one. It was as though she could track him across rooms. She'd been able to tell exactly when he left the B&B several hours earlier.

His absence should have reassured her, but it'd had the opposite effect. Now that he was gone, she felt more lost than ever. A part of her was missing right along with him.

Of course, she could not let that show.

It was ridiculous anyway. She hardly even knew the man.

"Maybe he's following a lead of his own tonight," Cooper offered. "Or maybe he's decided to sample the local nightlife. Poor sod, he's probably never even seen the inside of a club."

Jill rolled her eyes and opened the door to her room again.

"He may turn up by morning. Unless you wish to mount a search?" she asked Eric.

The latter shook his head. "It's probably nothing. Adam and I will stake out some shops on our own tonight, then we regroup in the morning."

Jill nodded and stepped inside, pulling the door shut behind her. She probably should have offered to drive the two bear shifters like she'd done previously, but she couldn't muster the energy. They'd be fine, surely. Now that Thomas had warned the burglars that Alpha Squad was onto them, they were unlikely to show themselves anyway.

The remaining squad members outside her room split up; footsteps could be heard walking away in all directions. Then, all that remained was deafening silence.

The inevitable had happened. The rest of the squad had noticed that one of their own was missing. Jill wasn't sure what would happen next. Would they suspect foul play?

She just had to play it cool, keep her head down. Maybe in time she'd be able to forget about what had happened. Then she'd move on with her life and do what she was best at: her job.

She fell back into the pillows and stared at the ceiling. It was too dark to see anything, but that didn't stop her from keeping her eyes open.

Deep breaths; in and out.

It was for the best, wasn't it? The mere thought of having to turn him in for what he'd done made her physically ill. Thanks to his betrayal, she'd found herself completely and utterly stuck.

Where had this misplaced loyalty on her part come from anyway? She'd been so hurt, even angry, when she found out about what Blackwood had done. And yet she couldn't *do* anything about it. Sending him away had been her only option.

They say the ones you love have the power to hurt you the most. Thomas Blackwood didn't deserve her love. So why was it that she still thought of him in those terms? What she'd felt for him had been a stupid immature crush, surely. One that came with weird Vulcan mind-meld type powers.

It had to be a shifter thing.

Jill remembered the awkward conversation she'd had with the major back on base, when it seemed like she was communicating with Eric without speaking aloud. Perhaps they had that kind of connection too. If they felt even a shred of what Jill had felt for Thomas before everything had gone wrong, she finally understood why the two had become a couple. No one, human or shifter, could possibly resist the temptation.

It made sense. Major Williams was a perfect role model otherwise, a strong woman who'd worked her way up the ranks within the British Military before taking on the herculean task of training and leading Alpha Squad. Jill had always respected the woman's professionalism and dedication to the job. Her indiscretions with Eric had seemed out of character.

But Jill understood now. She'd fallen into a similar trap with Blackwood.

Never again.

He was gone, and even though he was a traitor, Jill knew he would do his best to stick to his promise.

He wouldn't come back and make things worse for her, not after everything they'd felt together during the short moment they'd shared.

That chapter of her life was over.

She closed her eyes, took a deep breath, and waited for sleep to claim her.

It didn't.

Instead, she tossed and turned for what felt like all night. Until finally Jill woke up to the incessant screech of her alarm clock, without even remembering when she'd drifted off.

***

"Why would he just leave?" Adam mumbled, while taking a generous bite of toast and fried egg. Clearly, he wasn't worried enough to let it affect his appetite.

It would have been an amusing sight, if Jill didn't feel so empty this morning.

"Maybe he didn't leave voluntarily?" Cooper said.

"And last night's stake-out was a total waste of time as well," Adam added, in between mouthfuls of food. "It's like they knew we were there. They knew to lay low."

"Do you think they saw you?" Cooper asked.

Adam shrugged.

Eric, meanwhile, just sat there in the corner of the room, staring straight ahead, with a thoughtful yet stern expression on his face. Always the serious one.

Jill had nothing to add. No inputs, no comments. Every time she opened her mouth, she risked exposing herself, so she thought it best to keep quiet.

After what felt like forever, Eric finally spoke up. "We'll have to report this to Major Williams."

"Yes, we must," Jill agreed, feeling a bit sheepish that she hadn't come up with that herself.

Yet another example that she wasn't at her best lately, and especially not this morning.

"What are we going to tell her, though?" Adam wondered.

Jill kept her eyes fixed on Eric. He was in command. And anyway, he'd know just how to handle the major.

"Leave it to me," Eric said, scooting his chair back and getting up. He hadn't even touched his breakfast.

Neither had Jill.

"So, what are we thinking?" Cooper called after him. "Has he gone AWOL or has he deserted?"

Eric paused for but a moment. "We'll do what we do best. Investigate until we find out exactly what happened. It's too early to tell."

Jill exhaled deeply. If they uncovered the truth, this would go horribly wrong.

It was the right call though, that was the worst part about this. However little Eric had said, it was all spot on. Jill could kick herself for not being the one to make these suggestions.

Too late.

Eric exited the common room, leaving behind Adam, Cooper, herself, and one of the B&B's staff, who was replenishing the hot drinks buffet.

Today was going to be a long day.

Jill took a sip from her strong, black coffee and waited, with her eyes shut, for the caffeine to kick in. She hated the taste of black coffee, being more of a tea person, but she was desperate for the extra boost. For the first time in her entire professional life, she wished she could take the day off. Lounge in bed, watch mindless TV, anything to drown out the thoughts that kept going round and round in her head.

Unfortunately, she did not have this luxury.

"Well, this sucks," Cooper mumbled, and listlessly stabbed at the leftover food on his plate.

Jill wholeheartedly agreed with that assessment.

It was somewhat of a relief when Eric returned five minutes later, saving Jill and the rest of the squad from the awkward silence they'd descended into.

"New orders. Major Williams will join us over the weekend. Until then we are to steer the course. Keep investigating the crimes we were sent in here for. Keep Blackwood's disappearance under wraps for now without involving local law enforcement."

Jill nodded silently. It would be best not to air their dirty laundry in front of the locals.

"Finish up, everyone. We move out in ten," Eric ordered.

Efficient despite everything, they did, with Jill driving the squad vehicle as usual.

She could just about hear Eric address the other two team members in the back as she navigated her way through the small streets to the local police station.

"The Ministry of Shifter Affairs received an anonymous tip. Some suspicious activity going on near the railway line that runs along the northern part of town. No word on whether it's related to our case, but it's worth looking into," Eric said.

Jill blinked a few times, waiting for the light to change.

The Land Rover jerked ahead when she nervously released the clutch just a bit too quickly.

In Thomas's memories, she'd seen the place where he'd met with the renegade pack of wolves that seemed to be involved in the burglaries. They lived right next to the railway line. Coincidence? Probably not.

She exhaled slowly and tried to focus. So what if the squad was on the right track? Jill wasn't personally involved. Or was she?

Stop it! she thought to herself. *You're old and wise enough to make your own choices. And you chose to let Thomas go despite his crimes.*

The more she considered everything, the angrier it made her. Perhaps she should take on a more active role in this investigation. She hadn't brought Thomas to justice for what he'd done, but that didn't mean she couldn't do her part in bringing in the people who'd actually committed the burglaries. She'd chosen to let Thomas go because of the misplaced loyalty she felt for him. But there was no love lost between her and the real criminals.

At least *someone* should pay for their crimes. She would do her best to support the squad in making that happen.

The railway lines it is, then. Jill put her foot down and the Land Rover sped up. The sooner they could put this case behind them, the better.

Unfortunately, the best of intentions weren't enough to ensure their success.

When the squad Land Rover screeched to a halt on the unpaved track that led inside the wooded area where the suspicious activity had been reported, there was no sign of anyone there.

Fresh tire tracks and ashes littered the place. Someone had been here, and recently. Either they weren't very tidy, or they had left in a hurry, which meant that Alpha Squad once again found themselves empty handed.

"Whoever they were, they were wolves for sure," Adam remarked, inhaling deeply.

"What the hell? Why does this keep happening?" Cooper complained loudly as he looked around the abandoned campsite.

Adam shrugged. "Like they knew we were coming."

"Yeah… Exactly like they knew we were coming," Eric agreed.

Jill pressed her lips together. It looked like the case was far from over yet.

CHAPTER TEN

The more Thomas thought about this situation his loyalty to his uncle had landed him in, the more frustrated he became. After leaving the cafe in the morning, he'd continued to wander aimlessly without any clue where he was going. Walking seemed to make his mind run faster, though.

He'd come to a couple of clear conclusions.

Firstly, he had to make things right somehow. He had to correct his and Alpha Blackwood's mistake and catch the drifters before they went underground, never to be found again.

Secondly, if he was truly going to atone for his mistakes, he had to turn himself in.

Sure, the latter realization went against the promise he'd made to Jill, kind of. She'd asked him to leave, after all. But her reasons had been clear. They were mates; she could not endanger him even if she wanted to. So his presence on the squad meant that she'd be forced to keep his secrets.

If he turned himself in, that would solve her problem, so in a way he'd keep up his side of the deal; to make things easier on her. It was the only acceptable solution.

There was no way Thomas could live with himself if he didn't. He'd always had a strong sense of right and wrong.

And never before had his own actions pushed him so far across that boundary. He was no natural badass or outlaw.

After another full day of wandering the countryside, his feet had carried him to a place that smelled familiar. The scent of a fellow wolf dragged him out of his thoughts and back into reality. Whoever it was, he was very nearby…

"Who are you, and what are you doing here?" a stern voice asked.

Thomas flinched and turned around to confront the man. The wolf shifter Thomas came face-to-face with looked to be in his fifties. His weathered complexion and pale green eyes stood out against his greying black hair and full beard.

Everything about him, from his features to his accent, seemed vaguely familiar. It wasn't just that he was also a wolf, there was more to it.

"Thomas Blackwood," Thomas introduced himself, and stretched his hand out in an attempt at a greeting.

The man folded his arms and narrowed his eyes to slits. "What do you want?"

Thomas pulled his hand back again. Why was it that every fellow wolf he'd met outside of his hometown seemed completely unaware of the most basic niceties? Sure, the last one he'd met had been a despicable criminal who lived on the fringes of society, but what was this guy's excuse?

"I found myself in the area and was wondering if you

knew of any place where I might rest?" Thomas asked.

The man didn't answer, just continued to stare at him with his arms folded.

"Fine. You know what, never mind. I'll just continue walking, how about that? I've only come from Blackpool on foot. No big deal," Thomas complained.

"Look, lad. These are troubled times we live in," the man said. "And why is it that wolves are fleeing Blackpool in droves?"

"Excuse me?" Thomas asked.

"You're not the first wolf from Blackpool to ask for shelter here. Though you don't look or sound like them lot."

Thomas shook his head. "I'm not from Blackpool. I'm from Scotland."

"Figures. But what brings you here is what I want to know?"

"Tell me more about those other wolves who passed through here?" Thomas asked. "What did they look like?"

"Tall, ginger fellow and his underlings. They didn't smell right to me, so I sent them off."

It strangely made sense that during Thomas's own escape from Alpha Squad, he'd taken the same route that the drifters had taken to leave the heat of the law behind. Thomas had only followed instinct, taking the most natural route through the landscape, making the most amount of progress in the shortest amount of time to get as far away from Alpha Squad—and Jill—as possible.

"Were they also on foot?" Thomas asked.

The man laughed and ran his hand over his salt and pepper beard. "Not even close. They had a couple of cars and some camper vans. No, I must say, you're the only one I've seen in decades who's come this far on a hike."

"But you get a lot of people passing through here otherwise?" Thomas asked.

"If you don't know where you are, then why are you here?" The stranger cocked his head to the side.

"I… I'm not quite sure…" Thomas responded.

The man paused for a moment, then his expression softened a little. "Well, Thomas Blackwood from Scotland. Why don't you tell me a bit more about yourself? Then I'll decide what to do with you."

Thomas sighed. The long trek had taken its toll. He'd been so lost in thought throughout that he'd hardly noticed just how tired he was physically.

He'd been going non-stop since breakfast.

"What do you want to know?" Thomas asked.

"Where in Scotland?"

"Rannoch."

"Ah." The man paused. "Blackwood, you said? Any relation to Eric Blackwood?"

Thomas nodded. His alpha's reputation seemed to precede him wherever he went. "My uncle."

"I knew him once. Back when we were cubs. A remarkable man. Ambitious."

Thomas frowned. Was that the hint of familiarity he'd picked up on earlier? Was this guy also from his home town? He sure had traveled quite far himself to end up here.

"I suppose." Thomas ran his hand across his chin, which was starting to feel rough with the onset of stubble. He'd last shaved back at the B&B, over a day-and-a-half ago.

"You don't sound convinced?"

Enough with the questions already! He hadn't wanted to let anything slip, but it seemed not much got past this guy.

"I don't see how it's any of your business what I think." Thomas stared him straight in the eye.

The man smiled briefly and raised his hands in defense. "Hey, hey, each to their own. Now that we've established where you're from, please do tell me how you ended up here. We're a long way from Scotland."

Thomas shook his head. He didn't like where this was going at all. At this rate, he'd get himself into even more trouble without even trying.

"You have me at a disadvantage," Thomas said. "You now know who I am and where I'm from, down to my family history. But I still have no idea who *you* are!"

The man chuckled. "Alright, lad!"

This time *he* stretched out his hand, which Thomas shook reluctantly.

"James Ferguson."

Time for Thomas to eye him suspiciously. He'd heard

the name before. If only he could remember the context…

Thomas let go of his hand and continued to think.

"I left a bit before your time…" the man said, "From looking at the state of you, perhaps we might have had similar reasons."

Thomas opened his mouth to say something, but then closed it again. *That was highly unlikely.*

"I knew your uncle. We grew up together. When it was time for us to grow up and settle down, we had a—shall we say—*disagreement.*"

Thomas frowned again. "A disagreement?"

"Well, a lass had something to do with it too. That's just how it goes, isn't it?"

"Oh!" Thomas remarked. *Was he talking about Aunt Rebecca?*

James Ferguson smiled briefly. "It was around the time when the old alpha was starting to show signs of weakness. We were facing a leadership vacuum, and old boy Blackwood and I both tried to make a claim."

Thomas didn't need more detail than that to put two-and-two together. It was obvious how James's claim had turned out; if he'd won, it might have been Thomas's own uncle who left Rannoch. And who knew how things might have turned out then. If Thomas would have even met Jill, never mind betrayed and lost her forever.

"And why would you think that I left for the same reason?"

James grinned. "I can only assume that Eric Blackwood had something to do with your departure. Directly or indirectly. I can't imagine that he's suddenly adopted a hands-off leadership style after all these years. And you look as though you've recently gone through some woman trouble as well. I can practically smell the regret on you."

"So Alpha Blackwood exiled you after you lost?" Thomas asked. He wasn't even sure why he wanted to know.

"Oh, no, he was keen to keep me around. But I couldn't stand being there anymore. I didn't fancy bowing to anyone, especially not my childhood friend," James said.

Thomas found himself staring at the man in shock. He'd rejected the chance to serve his alpha. That was practically unheard of. James Ferguson was a very peculiar man indeed.

"I know, I know." James raised his hand in a calming motion. "I should have just been a good underling and done as I was told. But hey, something tells me you've got a bit of a rebellious streak in you too."

"Is that so?" Thomas asked.

"I could be wrong. But I really don't think I am."

Fair enough.

James stared at him for a moment, as though he was waiting for confirmation. Thomas wasn't about to give that to him. He couldn't be sure that he could trust him.

"So, those wolves who came by here earlier. Any idea where they would have gone?" Thomas asked instead.

James observed him in silence a little while longer.

Just when Thomas thought he wasn't going to get any more information out of the guy, he started to speak again.

"I suppose I could make a few calls."

"That would be very kind of you."

"Why don't you come inside while you wait," James suggested, and immediately turned around and started to walk.

Thomas had to hurry to keep up with him as they snaked up a small pathway leading away from the road, through an archway in a densely grown hedge, and finally paused in front of a modest little cottage, set back around five-hundred yards from the road in the quiet countryside.

"Here we are. Welcome to Ferguson's Rest Stop. Where you're free to stay as long as you like, as long as you leave your troubles at the gate." James gestured at the cozy cottage up the path.

Thomas frowned again. That was it! That was where he'd heard the name *James Ferguson* before!

"Shit, you're *the* James Ferguson?" Thomas blurted out.

James laughed so loudly it scared a few birds in a nearby tree. "Oh good, so you do know where you are now. I have to say, I was getting worried for a moment about how insular Rannoch had become since I left. I've worked long and hard to put this place on the map. What's the point if kids in my own hometown have never even heard of it?"

Thomas shook his head and took a good look around. He'd heard of the place, of course. Everyone had. Depending on who you asked, a million stories did the rounds about James Ferguson the outlaw, who chose to leave his pack and live outside of wolf laws and customs.

Parents would tell their young that if they misbehaved they'd send them to live at Ferguson's Rest Stop. As though it was wolf juvie. Meanwhile, by the time Thomas had reached his mid to late teens, the other kids in town would talk in hushed voices about how James Ferguson took in anyone who asked for refuge. That there were no rules at Ferguson's Rest Stop, and you could do whatever you wanted to there. It was *the* mythical drugs, sex, and rock 'n' roll destination of the wolf world.

Shocking to find out that James Ferguson was Rannoch bred himself. The older generation had really managed to hold on to that one secret.

"So if this is Ferguson's Rest Stop, and everyone's welcome, how come you sent the other group away?" Thomas asked finally.

James turned and grinned at him again. "They had trouble written all over them. I don't like trouble." He paused. "Was I wrong?"

Thomas returned his grin. "Not at all. Let me tell you all about it."

CHAPTER ELEVEN

By the time Sunday came around, Jill was grateful to get a little break from it all. Since Thomas's departure, she and the rest of the squad had done their best to track down any leads they got. Whether the tips had come in via the Ministry of Shifter Affairs, or the local police, none of them had led anywhere.

The burglars were long gone; Jill knew that. The rest of the squad was quickly catching on.

The only thing they didn't know was that they had Thomas Blackwood to thank for it.

Throughout the drive to Lauren's place, barely an hour away from Blackpool, Jill had done her best to ban all thoughts of Thomas from her mind. She'd also tried to swallow her frustration about the as yet unresolved burglary case.

A day—especially a birthday—with Lauren was difficult enough as it was.

She took a moment after parking the rental car in front of Lauren's house, tightly holding onto the steering wheel and gathering the courage to get out.

It'll be fine. Small talk and tea, that's all, she told herself.

A curtain twitched, prompting Jill into action. By the time she'd exited the vehicle, Lauren was already waiting at the door with two year old Harry on her hip.

"Jill!" Lauren squealed as Jill rushed up the front path.

She smiled as widely as she could manage under the circumstances and leaned in for a one-armed hug, making sure she didn't suffocate her nephew in the process.

"Happy birthday!" Jill said. "Hello, Harry!"

"Same to you, sis," Lauren answered.

She withdrew from the hug and took a step back.

"You look terrible, why don't you come inside." Lauren gestured eagerly.

"Uhh, thanks," Jill mumbled, while checking her face in the hallway mirror. The dark circles under her eyes were a bit obvious this morning. It didn't help that crying herself to sleep last night had left her eyelids reddish and slightly puffy.

"Kevin couldn't get time off work, so it's just the four of us today. You, me, Harry here, and little Caroline is having her late morning nap. But I'm sure we can entertain ourselves, can't we?"

"Great," Jill said. Too bad. It was awkward to admit, but Jill got on better with Kevin, her brother-in-law, than her very own sister. Considering they were twins, they'd always been surprisingly different as people.

Luckily, Lauren remained oblivious to Jill's true feelings. The last thing Jill needed today was another emotionally heavy exchange or even an argument. The past eighteen or so hours had been difficult enough as it was.

"I've baked us a cake," Lauren called out.

Jill followed her into the spacious open plan kitchen

cum dining room.

"Lovely. I could use some carbs," Jill said.

"Yeah, it looks like that."

Again with the looks! As if Jill was unaware of her current state.

"Work has been stressful," Jill explained, hoping they could leave that topic once and for all.

No such luck.

"You work too hard. I keep telling you, but you just won't listen. There are more things in life than work, you know!"

Lauren would know. She'd never held down a steady job in her entire life.

Jill suppressed a scoff.

"My career is important to me."

"Yeah… so you keep saying. All I'm saying is, how would you know if you don't try something else also?"

Things were going downhill quickly. And it was becoming increasingly difficult for Jill to bite her tongue.

"Tea?" Lauren suggested.

Finally, something Jill could fully get behind.

"Yes please."

Lauren put the toddler down in his play pen beside the dining table and put on the kettle.

Jill smiled awkwardly at the child, who'd started to chew on one of this stuffed toys. It wasn't that she didn't love her nephew, she was just still a bit uncomfortable around him.

That would change once he got a bit bigger and easier to communicate with.

As she watched the boy play on his own, she wondered if somehow she'd been born without the necessary instincts to be a mother. If maybe all those maternal instincts had only been passed on to Lauren instead of her.

"He's wonderful, isn't he?" Lauren asked while dropping a couple of tea bags into some mugs on the counter.

"Adorable." Jill forced a smile, then she diverted her attention to what Lauren was up to.

The freshly baked cake looked promising. Perhaps the impending sugar rush would put Jill into a better mood.

She waited while Lauren zipped around the kitchen, locating a couple of plates and a cake server. It was dizzying to watch her.

Finally, Lauren joined Jill at the table.

Jill raised her mug. "To us, on our birthday."

"To family," Lauren corrected her.

The moment the hot liquid touched Jill's tongue, she lost the will to argue back.

"Seriously, I think you need to take some time for yourself," Lauren said.

Jill looked up to find her sister's eyes already on her.

Didn't she know it. But what could she do? The squad needed her, especially now that they were in a panic over Blackwood's sudden departure. She couldn't just let them down. She was the reason he'd left in the first place!

"Maybe find a nice man to settle down with? I thought it would never happen for me, until I met Kevin. My entire worldview changed."

Jill felt her throat close up. The suggestion that she, or any woman for that matter, needed a man to lead a happy, complete life, nauseated her. She wasn't like that. She might not be a classic feminist with the attitude to show for it, but she considered herself an independent woman. That was why she had joined the military, something Lauren had never understood.

But the sad part was… *Ever since Thomas…*

She put her mug down and took a deep breath.

It was no use.

Her eyes were already burning, the inside of her chest stinging so badly it was as though she was being stabbed by a thousand knives from the inside out. In her military career, she'd been physically hurt before. She'd been in a car accident once, and woken up in a hospital bed with searing pain stabbing into her legs.

None of it compared to what she felt now. Heartache was a real, tangible thing.

"What's wrong?" Lauren asked.

Jill pressed her lips together and just shook her head. *No.* She wouldn't let herself down like this. She wouldn't allow herself to crack.

But it was too late.

Before she knew it, she let out a loud, miserable sob which startled little Harry, causing him to cry as well.

"Oh Lauren, I've messed up so bad!" Jill cried. "He was right there. Sure, things weren't perfect, but are they ever? I sent him away, made him promise he wouldn't come back. He's the sort of guy who'll actually do it too. Just because I told him."

The more she spoke about Thomas, the more she wanted to continue. To tell Lauren of their kiss, that little slice of heaven she'd experienced, just before everything had fallen apart.

She blinked through her tears and found Lauren staring at her with her mouth agape.

"What on earth are you on about?" Lauren mumbled.

"A guy! On the squad!"

Lauren continued to look stunned.

That shouldn't have come as a surprise to Jill. In all of thirty years that they'd walked this earth, Jill had never once opened up quite like this. Of course, nothing nearly as significant had ever happened to her either, but still.

She sniffled, loudly, and watched as Lauren picked up Harry and tried to comfort him.

What the hell was wrong with her? There were no words to explain how she felt or what exactly had happened. What was she going to tell Lauren, that there was a guy—a werewolf, no less—who'd somehow tapped into her thoughts and emotions to the extent that they could basically communicate telepathically? That she'd felt what he felt, seen what he'd seen?

Lauren would never believe it. It would blow her reality apart.

Jill wrapped her hands around the mug of still steaming tea and kept them there until her palms burned.

This wasn't the time or the place.

The flow of tears down her cheeks was starting to slow.

"Never mind. I think I'm overworked or something," Jill mumbled.

"That's what I've been trying to tell you," Lauren said meekly, handing her a tissue.

Jill took it and dabbed it against her eyes before blowing her nose in it.

No, this won't do . Whatever had happened with Thomas was her problem to deal with, not Lauren's.

She forced a very tentative, miserable smile. "How about that cake, then?"

Lauren nodded, the shock still evident on her face. "Yes, cake… you go ahead, I'd better put little Harry down for his nap now."

Jill waited until Lauren had rushed out of the room, then she rested her head in her hands. What a disaster. This had to be the worst birthday ever. How could things get any worse?

———— ♦ ————

By the time Jill survived the remainder of her birthday meet-up with Lauren and reached the B&B in Blackpool, she discovered that things *could* get worse.

The major was there, waiting.

"Where have you been, Private?" she demanded.

Jill felt all the air leave her chest instantly. "Uhh, birthday… at my sister's, Ma'am?"

The major's expression softened. "Oh, your day off. I'm sorry, I totally forgot."

Jill relaxed slightly, allowing herself to breathe again. "No problem."

"Join us in the common room as soon as possible. It's important you're there for this," the major instructed.

"Yes, ma'am."

Jill's heart was racing once again, and her head was pounding. Obviously the major wasn't happy about Thomas's disappearance, or was there something more?

She quickly dumped her bag inside her room and changed out of her civilian clothes.

When she made it to the common room, she noted that Adam, Cooper, and Eric were already there. And the major, of course.

"We're all here. Wonderful," the major started.

Jill swallowed hard when she felt everyone's eyes on her. Still, she forced her shoulders back in an attempt to look more confident than she felt. The guilt was getting to her. Had they figured it out?

"Thomas Blackwood's disappearance raises a number

of questions we do not yet have an answer to. There was no sign of struggle or any evidence in his room indicating he left against his will, only that he packed in a rush. There was no note or anything to explain his actions."

Jill caught herself holding her breath.

"He was a likeable guy. We've all worked with him for six months now, but we must resist the urge to let our shared history color our perception of the case now. We must ask difficult questions, even if we do not really want to."

From the corner of her eye, Jill noticed Cooper had raised his hand.

"Yes?" the major addressed him.

"Ma'am," he started. "I'm not sure I understand. Are you trying to say that he might have permanently quit the squad?"

The major scanned the room, her eyes lingering on each of the squad members for a few seconds, before moving on to the next. Jill felt her chest tighten when she moved into the major's cross hairs.

"I want to ask you all a question. Does anyone else find it strange that after a crime spree that has shown no signs of slowing for weeks now, we haven't seen further activity from these burglars we were sent in to investigate? Almost as if someone warned them? And then, shortly after Blackwood's disappearance, you locate the burglars' hideout, only to find that all of them left in a hurry?"

Jill tried to swallow her rising panic, but it went all wrong, causing her to cough violently.

"Sorry," she croaked, when she felt everyone's eyes on her, still trying to get her breathing back under control.

"You think Blackwood had something to do with it? That he might be involved somehow?" Cooper asked, his eyes wide with shock.

"I'm not ready to jump to conclusions. But I want us to investigate the possibility," the major said.

This was a nightmare.

Jill's cheeks were burning after her coughing fit. She was certain her face would be bright red by now.

"Agreed. We must run down all possible scenarios," Eric chimed in.

Adam sat in silence with a contemplative frown on his face.

"I'm glad we're all on the same page," the major said, eying Jill once more. "I just wish that we could get our hands on at least one of the thieves so that we might question him and find out for sure if Blackwood had a hand in any of this."

The mere thought filled her with dread, but Jill nodded in agreement. What else could she do?

CHAPTER TWELVE

Come nightfall, Thomas was getting ready to leave James Ferguson's house with only one goal in mind: he had to somehow catch up with the drifters. Luckily for him, they weren't on the run.

After failing to find refuge at Ferguson's Rest Stop, they'd stopped at the next convenient place. Word of several young families moving into a campsite a few towns over was already starting to spread. Nothing traveled faster than small town gossip.

The wannabe outlaws had no clue what was coming in their way.

Thomas wasn't just fueled by the need to make things right with the squad. He was first and foremost doing this for Jill. To at least try to make up for letting her down earlier.

After telling James the whole sordid tale so far, Thomas had gained an ally. He couldn't be sure if James's willingness to help him was motivated at least in part by his desire to undermine Alpha Blackwood. Thomas didn't care much about his reasons; he was just grateful for the help.

So it was that Thomas ended up in James's car, with the latter behind the wheel.

"I know the place a bit. If you're careful, you'll be able

to get in and out without the management finding out," James said.

Thomas nodded. "It would be best to do this with as little interference as possible."

"I could create a diversion?" James suggested. "While you round them up one by one, starting with their leader."

That could work.

They drove the rest of the way in silence, with Thomas wondering what it would be like to face Jill again after this was all over. One way or another, he was going to end things tonight. At least one prisoner. That was his baseline.

If he got just one of them and managed to transport him back to Blackpool, Thomas would turn himself in too.

"Here we are." James nodded at the gate, straight ahead. "This time of year, the site should be mostly empty."

"I'll be able to sniff them out, don't worry."

"Good luck, son. Make 'em pay."

Thomas turned and smiled briefly at James.

"You never told me why you decided to help," Thomas said.

James shook his head. "I don't like it when people abuse their position."

So his assumption had been correct. James only did it to spite his old rival, Alpha Blackwood.

"I can respect that. I don't like that either," Thomas agreed.

James nodded. "Well. Break a leg."

Thomas grinned. *Let's hope it doesn't come to that.* He opened his door and slipped out of the car with hardly a sound. Almost immediately, Thomas broke into a sprint, running along the edge of the woods that lined the driveway. He let his nose lead him the rest of the way, continuing to stick to the unlit parts of the site.

James was right; as he made it into the heart of the campsite, he could see that the vast majority of pitches were unoccupied.

A small cluster of campers stood off to the far edge, again, near some woods. Light flickered in one of the windows, and the rest were dark. His nose hadn't let him down. The scent of wolf in the air was unmistakable.

Thomas sneaked up to the first caravan, the one with the lights on inside. The low murmur of a television could be heard from near the window. He tiptoed and peeked inside. Although the small TV in the corner was flickering, the armchair facing it was empty.

What the hell?

"Well, well, if it isn't the Boy Scout from Rannoch," a voice spoke up behind him. He froze for a second as adrenaline flooded his system. Then he turned, slowly, with his hands up.

"Hi, I was wondering if you might help me," Thomas started.

He recognized the young man as one of the wolves he'd seen at the drifter camp near the railway line. He might have lost the element of surprise, but at least he'd located his target.

"Help? What for?" the man asked.

Thomas was desperate for his brain to feed him something of use. Anything would do.

A loud crash echoed through the mostly empty lot.

The other wolf turned instantly to see where the sound had come from. At that moment, Thomas could hear James's voice bellowing across the field, near the campsite office and restaurant.

"Bastards, all of ya! Think you can take my farm from me, huh? I'm not going to let it happen, I won't!"

Thomas frowned. So James's idea of a distraction was to make a spectacle of himself? The man never ceased to surprise.

"What the…" The wolf turned to face Thomas again. "You know what that's all about?"

Thomas shrugged. Good thing he'd had no idea of James's plan before, so at least he didn't need to pretend to be surprised.

"Whatever it is, he sounds pretty riled up," Thomas said.

Right on cue, James Ferguson started ranting and raving again. That it was *his land* and nobody should dare to take it from him or he'd have his head. He was a great actor, it seemed.

Thomas could hear another voice also, another man who was trying to calm James down.

"Look, mate. I think you might have had a few too many…" the other man said.

"Yeah…" The young wolf turned again and stared at where the ruckus was coming from, giving Thomas his chance.

He allowed the shift to come over him, and pounced. His opponent never knew what hit him. By the time he tried to react, Thomas had already managed to transform back into his human self and put a pair of handcuffs on him.

"You lying bastard!" he shouted. "You were meant to help us!"

The lights in the other two campers switched on as well, and the curtain on the nearer one twitched. Thomas could just about make out two large, fearful eyes. It was the young woman he'd seen earlier. The one with the child.

He wouldn't have long. Thomas swiftly dragged his prisoner to the empty caravan and forced him inside, blocking the door with one of the heavy wooden picnic tables that seemed to belong to the campsite itself.

At the same time, the door of the other caravan swung open and the pack leader appeared. He looked like a wild man. His unruly reddish hair, back lit by the yellow glow from the interior of the caravan, gave the impression of being on fire.

"What the hell is going on out here?" he shouted, then he spotted Thomas, as well as his underling, lying tied up on the ground.

He reacted instantly. His skin sprouted reddish brown fur, and his limbs and spine twisted and morphed until he had taken on his final shape. It was all over in just a second, but Thomas was ready for him.

He followed suit, letting his wolf take over, and charged at his opponent. The two of them rolled around on the ground, snapping and snarling at each other. Each got a few good hits in, until Thomas finally managed to get a good grip on the drifter's neck. The latter bucked and continued to fight, despite the life-threatening position he found himself in.

Thomas didn't back down either. He put his full weight on top of the red wolf, pinning him to the ground, until he could do little other than yelp in pain. Then, in the blink of an eye, he forced the beast back into the shadows and emerged, fully human, wielding another pair of handcuffs.

"Gotcha," Thomas said, as he hauled the restrained wolf off the ground and cuffed him to a sturdy metal railing on the outside of the caravan.

All the combat training he'd undergone as part of Alpha Squad had really paid off.

A low growl distracted him. He looked up to find four more of the wolves he'd first come across in Blackpool forming a semi-circle around him.

"Look. I've taken down your alpha. If you want the same sort of treatment, be my guest," Thomas hissed.

"What are you waiting for?" their alpha complained.

"Get me out of these bloody cuffs!"

One lunged forward, his fist raised, as though he was planning on knocking Thomas out. He ducked, just at the right moment, causing the young lad to stumble a few steps ahead.

Thomas grabbed hold of him by the collar and yanked him back. At this rate, he'd need more handcuffs.

The remaining youngsters just watched. Thomas had already taken down their alpha, as well as their more impulsive compatriot. That did not bode well for the rest of them.

"What's going on here, then?" a familiar voice called out.

Thomas couldn't suppress a grin as James Ferguson marched right into the stand-off between Thomas and the rest of the drifter pack.

The young wolves moved aside, letting James pass.

"You're joking! You're a bunch of cowards, you are!" their alpha raged.

They seemed to be weighing their options. Sure, they still had the numbers, but Thomas had just shown his superiority by taking down two of their own in record time. The arrival of a well-known fellow wolf who seemed to have taken Thomas's side only complicated things for the drifters.

These were followers, not leaders. And they had just run out of options.

As a result, they all seemed to make up their minds at roughly the same time.

Two fled straight across the empty campsite, and disappeared down the drive that led to the main road.

"Keep an eye on the prisoners," Thomas called out.

James nodded, leaving Thomas to chase after the other one, who sprinted around the cluster of caravans and into the woods that lay behind. He was incredibly fast, forcing Thomas to undergo yet another transformation to continue his pursuit.

It was no use, though. All he achieved was to deplete the rest of his energy for the night.

Three out of five wasn't bad, right?

Thomas returned to the campers, only to find that James had taken up residence inside the camper where Thomas had locked up the first prisoner.

"Alright?" Thomas asked. "Hope your distraction didn't end too badly."

James waved Thomas's question away. "Ah, the proprietor here is a mate of mine. He thought it was a right laugh. Here, come and take a look at this!"

Thomas joined James in front of the small television. Images of Blackpool appeared on screen.

"…live from Blackpool this evening, where the local police have arrested a local wolf shifter who was caught robbing a petrol station. Jenny, you're on the scene right now. What can you tell us?"

Thomas stood back and folded his arms. A million

things were going through his mind.

What timing. Right when he'd caught up with the entire gang, what were the odds of the police catching one who'd stayed behind in Blackpool?

"I'm going to take this as a sign," Thomas said.

"Oh yes?" James asked.

"Yeah. That no matter what Alpha Blackwood wanted, these clowns were meant to get caught. All of them. Sooner or later, the ones that got away will get themselves into trouble too and the law will catch up with them."

James chuckled. "You really hold on to a grudge, don't you? Look, you've done a good thing here. You've done your job, brought the ringleader and two of his underlings in. But don't forget, you're not so different from them in a way."

Thomas scoffed. "No way. I'm nothing like these boys!"

James grinned and shook his head. "Remember, only days ago, you were ready to blindly follow your alpha's orders, without considering the right or wrong of it at all."

Thomas wanted to argue. That he would never resort to robbing jewelry stores on his alpha's say-so. He didn't, though. As much as he hated to admit it, James did have a point. His actions this past week had earned him at least a bit of a lecture.

"So you think I should let them go?" Thomas asked.

James shrugged. "That's up to you. But I can't imagine

they're all that bad. They just haven't had the best start in life."

"So if they come knocking on your door, will you let them in?" Thomas asked.

James laughed. "Oh well, that entirely depends. Only if they're willing to leave their troubles behind at the gate."

The triumphant tone in which James repeated his motto made Thomas chuckle, despite everything.

"Okay, fair enough. I suppose thanks are in order," he said. "I couldn't have pulled this off without you."

"No need. I was glad to be of help to a fellow wolf from Rannoch."

"Cheers," Thomas said. "You going to help me get these prisoners back to Blackpool?"

James leaned forward and picked up a bunch of keys from the shelf beside the TV.

"I'll help you load them into a car, but then I'd better get home. In my line of work, I find it best to stay away from the police as much as I can."

James got up and gave Thomas a manly pat on the shoulder.

"Good luck, son. And if you do happen to speak to your aunt Rebecca, give her my best, will you?"

So he *had* been after her too once upon a time.

"Will do."

CHAPTER THIRTEEN

"I ain't talking to you." The boy—he couldn't have been much older than late teens—folded his arms and stared straight ahead, ignoring Eric King, who had taken a seat in front of him inside one of the local police station's interrogation rooms.

Jill observed the entire scene from behind the one-way glass of the observation area. Beside her sat Detective Tate, the local in charge of the entire investigation. It was a small room, meaning the rest of the squad, including Major Williams, was forced to wait outside.

When the police had called the previous evening to notify Alpha Squad that they'd caught a wolf who was running away after robbing a petrol station, Jill found herself torn yet again. On the one hand, she was thrilled that one of the burglars had potentially been caught, but on the other hand…

There was something unpredictable about the boy. Like his loyalties could shift in a flash and he'd sell everyone he knew down the river with him. Including Thomas Blackwood.

What if he knew all about Thomas and his affiliations with Alpha Squad? Had he been there when Thomas had warned the rest of his crew?

Around the kid hung the sort of vibe that suggested he

did not care what bridges he burned, as long as he got even the slightest benefit out of it. And anyway, why was it that he'd stayed behind to let himself get caught when the rest of his pack had seemingly vanished overnight?

"No matter. You can listen instead," Eric said.

The two shifters stared each other down, until finally the boy averted his gaze.

Jill wasn't as well versed in shifter body language as perhaps she liked to be, but she could tell that they were establishing the pecking order. And the boy had just lost.

The painful experience with Thomas had taught Jill that wolves were generally more respectful of authority figures than bears seemed to be. Thomas had betrayed his personal values to serve his alpha after all, apparently without questioning his orders much.

Jill opened a fresh page on her notepad and waited, pen in hand, for the boy to say or do something worthy of making it into her report.

"You were caught in the act. The local police have you on CCTV, shifting, then running away from the scene of a crime."

The boy scoffed and stared at the blank wall to Eric's left. His hand instinctively reached for his shoulder, where the police had tased him during the arrest. There was simply no other way for humans of average size and strength to capture a shifter safely; Jill knew this.

"So I'm not questioning you to find out if you did it. We already know. You're already going down for this robbery. And the law doesn't take kindly to threatening people with a weapon, so the punishment will be severe," Eric said.

"What weapon? I didn't have no weapon!" the boy protested.

Oh God, Eric got him talking. Jill's heart sank. Who knew what else he might say now? Why couldn't this whole wretched affair just be over already?

"You shifted in front of the petrol pump clerk. Teeth and claws, mate. Those count as weapons under new law."

"That's just my face. What do I do 'bout it? I got excited, accidentally shifted, so what?"

Eric folded his hands. "It makes no difference. Teeth are teeth, and you went and showed yours to a defenseless human."

The boy smirked and looked away again. "So what do you want then?"

"I want to know where the rest of your group has gone."

"I dunno. If I did, I wouldn't tell the likes of you, neither."

"Fine. Have it your way. But if I were you, I'd think twice about refusing to help us. It's no fun being locked in a concrete box, which is where you'll be spending a very long time indeed, unless you help us find the rest of your pack."

"Makes no difference to me," the boy said.

Jill made some general notes about his demeanor, as well as the minor admissions Eric had managed to coax out of him. At least he seemed to be holding out so far. Or perhaps he had no idea about who Thomas was and what he'd done.

A commotion outside interrupted Jill's thoughts. Detective Tate got up out of his chair to see what was going on. That was when Jill felt *him*.

Thomas Blackwood was outside.

She panicked. After making him promise he'd stay away, what the hell was he doing back here? Jill knocked her chair over on the way out and waited in the open doorway, observing the scene outside.

There he stood, in the center of the police station, surrounded by uniformed cops and the remaining members of Alpha Squad. Everyone was talking at the same time, making it impossible to understand a word.

Next to him stood an angry looking red-haired man, with his hands cuffed in front of him.

What are you doing? Jill thought. *Who is that?*

Thomas looked up and made eye contact with her.

I am here to make things right.

Jill frowned. *And how are you going to explain what happened to Major Williams? To the rest of the squad?*

Thomas smiled briefly. *I intend to tell the truth. They deserve to know.*

A lump developed in Jill's throat. He wasn't a bad guy after all; the same urge to do the right thing and do his job that had inspired his return had led him astray earlier. Despite everything, his heart was in the right place.

But just because Jill had realized this now didn't change things. If he followed through, the fallout would be disastrous.

Jill observed the detective in charge and some of his colleagues. They hadn't been too pleased with Alpha Squad's involvement. If they discovered that a squad member had sabotaged their case, it wouldn't matter that Thomas had come forward himself. The bad press would harm the squad and undermine the good work they'd done so far. Secretary Teese would be furious. General Stone at the base would get his greatest wish; the writing would be on the wall for the squad.

Meanwhile, Thomas would be feeding himself to the wolves, no pun intended.

There was only one way out of this, for all of them.

You can't tell them. Think of what it'll do to the squad! Jill thought. *Follow my lead.*

"Blackwood! You're back," Jill raised her voice. "I see your mission has been successful?"

Thomas blinked a few times, then nodded slowly. "Yes, I managed to arrest the figurehead behind all these break-ins we've been investigating. Here he is."

The man standing to Thomas's left angrily stared at the crowd surrounding him. Thankfully, he kept his mouth shut.

Major Williams stepped forward and exchanged a few hushed words with Thomas.

"Explain yourself," Jill heard her say.

Tell her you went undercover.

The major would be unhappy with Thomas going off on his own without telling the rest of the squad, but that wasn't nearly as dangerous as telling her the truth. In a way, he could pretend he was following her orders to take on a more proactive role. Sort of.

"I saw an opportunity to infiltrate the pack. To gain their trust," Thomas spoke in a hushed tone. "There simply wasn't time to run it by anyone."

Jill smiled to herself. *Yes!* She'd planted the seed of the story in his mind, and he was running with it. With a bit of luck, this was the way out that they so desperately needed.

"I should have known not to trust you. Eric Blackwood and his entire clan can go to hell as far as I'm concerned." The cuffed man beside him glared at Thomas in anger. It struck Jill just how icy cold his eyes were.

So at least one person in the room believed the story. Jill glanced at Major Williams, who had her back towards her now.

"We're not done talking about this," the major whispered.

Thomas nodded.

Then the major turned and eyed Jill, who felt a cold chill run down her spine. She was onto them. How?

"Detective Tate. Why don't you take this man into

custody, process him, see if you can learn anything to solve your case," Major Williams spoke as she turned away from Jill again.

The detective did not look convinced. He rested both his hands on his hips. "What evidence have you got against this man?"

Thomas patted the right pocket on his tactical vest, then he slipped his hand inside and retrieved two see-through plastic bags.

"I think you'll find this particular watch on the insurance inventory of the jewelry store on Church Street. The one that was hit recently," Thomas said. "And this fur sample might be of use in case you wish to do a DNA test. I found it at the same crime scene."

"Is that all you found?" one of the other policemen chimed in. "Because that's not enough. The chain of custody—"

"Oh, there's more," Thomas interrupted him. "It seems that they left town in such a hurry they never had the chance to fence their haul."

The detective and the other policeman exchanged a few hushed words, while Major Williams stood beside Thomas with her arms folded. This was one of the things Jill admired about the major. She had her doubts about Thomas's explanation, but she'd never show it in front of outsiders.

"By the way, there are a couple more people in my car,

outside," Thomas added.

Jill bit her lip and waited for someone—anyone—to say something to break the tension. *You've been busy since you've been gone.*

Thomas winked at her. *Let's say I was extremely motivated to correct my mistakes.*

"Very well. Clark, Kendrick! Why don't you see in the remaining prisoners," Detective Tate said, glancing first at Thomas, then at Major Williams. "Meanwhile, we made an arrest of our own. Let's see if these two know each other."

Jill held her breath as the crowd, led by Detective Tate and the prisoner, started walking toward the interrogation room. Thomas's prisoner let out a whole stream of expletives as soon as the detective revealed who sat on the other side of the door.

"You bloody fool! Why couldn't you just do what you were told for once?" he ranted.

"Why? So that I could get caught right along with you? I took a chance on my own. So what?" the youngster retorted.

Jill could hardly suppress a smile.

"Well, then. That answers that question." Detective Tate yanked the red-haired man back out of the interrogation room and handed him over to two of his uniformed colleagues. "I suppose congratulations are in order."

Thomas shrugged.

This is so awkward. I barely know what to say to these people. I hate having to lie.

Jill pressed her lips together. It made sense. From the moment this whole mission had started, Thomas had been battling two important values he'd always tried to live by.

Follow orders , and *be truthful.*

That was why he'd acted so guilty; this disconnect had threatened to tear him up inside.

Just smile and nod. It'll pass soon enough, Jill thought. *I need you to survive this. And this is the only way.*

Luckily, the police and the rest of the squad were too busy inspecting the evidence and processing and interrogating all the people Thomas had brought in to pay any more attention to him. For now.

CHAPTER FOURTEEN

Thomas couldn't believe what had just happened. He'd marched the first of his prisoners into the local police station, ready to face the music, and instead, Jill had turned the entire situation around and made him look like a hero.

He didn't feel like one.

He didn't deserve to be let off the hook for what he'd done.

Once the prisoners had been processed, and the detective had questioned Thomas for a bit, getting his side of the story—well, Jill's version of events—he was glad to leave the bustling police station behind. Who knew how much longer he could keep up the charade.

Once the entire squad was back at the B&B, it turned out that Major Williams wasn't as easily convinced as the police had been. She took both Thomas and Jill aside for a private conversation, away from the rest of the squad in a quieter part of the B&B.

"You know how I feel about squad members going off on their own," she said. "We're supposed to be a team."

Thomas nodded, keeping his gaze fixed on the ground.

Just stick to the story, he could hear Jill's voice in his head.

Ever since that first kiss, only a couple of days ago, it had been a revelation how seamlessly they communicated together. That didn't make lying any easier, but at least he knew he wasn't alone.

"I'm sorry, Ma'am. These wolves are a suspicious bunch. They would have never opened up to me if they knew I worked with humans and bear shifters on the same squad," he said.

"Right." The major diverted her attention to Jill.

"And you knew about this, Private?" she asked.

Jill shot Thomas a quick look, then nodded. "I had my suspicions, Ma'am."

"And you didn't feel it necessary to notify the rest of the squad? To notify me? I'm highly disappointed."

Thomas felt his entire body tense up. Major Williams was their superior, and hence it was well within her rights to reprimand them. But he found it hard to ignore the urge to protect Jill.

We'll be fine. What is she going to do, fire us? After a win like this? Jill tried to reassure him. He could sense that she was a bundle of nerves herself, though.

"I... I couldn't be sure until he came back," Jill stammered.

"I'm not happy, I'll tell you that right now. But at least things worked out."

"It was for the good of the mission," Jill said, her voice so low it was almost a whisper.

"The mission, yes. Well, Secretary Teese will be pleased to find out that the burglars have been caught."

The major folded her arms and looked first at Jill, then

back at Thomas. She sighed deeply and shook her head.

"What am I going to do with you two?" she mumbled, as though she was talking to herself.

"I'm sorry?" Jill asked.

"There's something you're not telling me. I know there is," the major concluded.

Thomas pressed his lips together and stared straight ahead at a faded painting hanging on the wall opposite him.

She knows we're hiding something because she has secrets of her own, Jill thought.

What secrets? Thomas shot her a questioning look, then he caught himself and looked at the ugly painting again.

"Anyway, I haven't got time for this right now. I'd like to be back on base by night fall. Private, you can drive the squad vehicle back tomorrow morning," the major said. "Dismissed."

"Thank you Ma'am," Jill said.

Thomas just nodded; his mind was still elsewhere.

Go on, what secrets? he thought.

Jill looked up and watched as Major Williams left.

Eric King and her; they're a couple.

Thomas turned and watched the major as she vanished around the corner at the end of the hall.

"Impossible!"

Jill nodded. "Yes. That's how she knows we're not being truthful. She can recognize how we are together."

Thomas inhaled sharply through his teeth. "And here I

thought we were unique. I've never known another mixed couple."

"So how does this work, anyway? Us," Jill asked. "The thoughts, the feelings. It's all so… different."

Footsteps coming up the hallway prompted Thomas to keep quiet.

I'll tell you all about it once we're truly alone.

Jill smiled and nodded, and they hurried down the hall, away from the noises he'd just heard, until they reached his room.

Here was where everything had truly begun. The first moment he'd realized that she felt the same about him. When he knew that they were meant to be after all, and it wasn't just a pathetic obsession on his part.

Their first kiss…

He wanted a second one. And a third, plus many more. Enough to last a lifetime.

But there was still something that bothered him.

You didn't need to intervene back at the station, you know. I was ready to accept the consequences of my actions, Thomas thought, gazing into Jill's eyes. Now more than ever, she managed to captivate him.

Incorrect; I had no choice. And you know why. She stared back at him, a subtle smile playing on her lips.

He did. *I just wish you didn't have to lie for me.*

Jill shook her head and averted her gaze, however briefly. *I'm used to keeping secrets. It comes with the job. All I've done is bent the truth just slightly to help things along a bit. Otherwise where would you be now? And what about the rest of the squad?*

Thomas reached for her hand and gently caressed it with his thumb. How small and fragile she felt under his touch. So many surprises in such a petite package.

I guess I'd be in jail, Thomas concluded.

And the squad would be facing its worst PR crisis ever. Now instead, we're all still here and you're still a part of the team. That's what you want, right? To continue to work together. To make a difference.

Thomas thought for a moment. She was right. He'd rebelled against his alpha, so going back to Rannoch would no longer be an option; not unless he wanted to barge in, guns blazing, and make a claim to become alpha himself. That wasn't something he was interested in.

No, nostalgia aside, the outside world was a much more exciting place to be than his home town.

That meant that all he had left was this squad.

And her.

Mostly her.

I wasn't ready to be in love with a jailbird, I'll tell you that right now, Jill thought.

He wanted to touch her more intimately. To show her how torn up he'd been about her these past few days, but mostly to show her how much she meant to him.

Jill took a step in his direction and closed her eyes. He reached for her and slipped his hand around her neck.

Back to my question, Jill thought. *What happens now? To us?*

He smiled and pulled her closer to him until her small frame was pressed up against him. *Whatever we want. Wolves mate for life. This connection is the reason you couldn't stand by and see me get into trouble . I am yours, as you are mine.*

Jill's eyes became moist. Thomas might have missed it if her face wasn't this near to his.

I never thought this would happen for me. That I'd have to choose between my career and love. And I did *make a choice last week, the wrong one. Still, here you are.*

Her admission made his heart ache. He wrapped his arms around her shoulder and back and drew her against him tighter. She was so small, so precious. He could sacrifice himself to protect her. He almost did, too. He would have turned himself in for her. Instead she went and flipped everything around.

I guess we both made mistakes, huh? Thomas thought.

Never again. I'm not ready to let you go again, she responded.

Jill tiptoed, lifting her face up toward his. He leaned down and gave in to sweet temptation.

This second kiss was as glorious, if not more so, than the first. Emotion overload.

Their minds fully opened up again, just like that first time. Their thoughts became one, as did their memories.

He experienced everything she'd been through while he was away. The constant fear of the squad finding out the truth. The terrible visit to her sister's place on Sunday.

"Belated happy birthday," Thomas whispered, between kisses.

Jill smiled into his lips. "It is now."

He picked her up into his arms and carried her across the room to the bed, where he gently set her down again.

She let out a soft giggle as she sank into the mattress, with him crawling on top of her. More kisses were needed. All the pain, all the grief he'd caused her—he wanted to make it all better. This was the only way his instincts knew how.

"If I didn't feel so utterly helpless, I'd tell you to at least buy me dinner first," Jill whispered, as she writhed up against him.

"Sure. Anything for you," Thomas mumbled, though he made no effort to stop what he was doing.

She started to fumble with the buttons on his shirt, opening them one by one with trembling fingers.

He looked down and saw the same passion in her eyes that he felt in his heart. She'd ignited something in him. The drive to be better. An improved version of himself. To stick to his principles, and do the best possible job he could.

Thanks to her, he had a second chance on the squad and in life. If that wasn't worth fighting for, nothing was.

She reached for him and pulled him down on top of her while slipping her hands underneath his shirt.

It was too much. His wolf took over.

He pulled back and tore the remainder of his uniform

off in one swift move. If the major or anyone had a problem, he'd say it happened during a fight or transformation.

She did her best to catch up, unbuttoning herself and slipping first one, then the other arm out of her shirt. She opened her trousers next, gesturing at him to do the rest.

Thomas tugged at both legs, pulling them off her and dropping them halfway across the room.

The sight of her in those skimpy little underpants and bra on his bed drove him wild, as did her scent. They were both well beyond the regular rules of courtship. Nature had taken over. He could smell the lust on her, but he still held back.

What was he waiting for? Was he just savoring the moment, or asking for permission?

Thank you for everything, he thought. *I'll make sure you never regret this.*

Jill smiled up at him and readjusted her position, resting one foot on the mattress beside her, with her knee in the air.

"Make me yours," she whispered.

He didn't need to hear that twice.

"Yes, Ma'am," he said, and pounced.

CHAPTER FIFTEEN

Once again, Jill couldn't explain what had come over her. From the moment Thomas had left—at her insistence, no less—she'd been walking around like her life was over. Then when he came back, all that attraction that had soured when she found out about his secret mission was back with a vengeance.

It didn't seem to matter anymore what he'd done.

All that mattered was that he was back, giving her a second chance with him.

She should have never sent him away in the first place. It had seemed like the rational thing to do; the next best thing after turning him in to the major or the police, which she seemed physically incapable of.

Thing was, the way she felt about him didn't leave room for rational thought.

So after coming up with that plan to smooth things over with the squad, she inevitably ended up in his room again.

And things naturally progressed from there.

Jill was naked on her back.

It should have been awkward, falling into bed with this man. It should have bothered her, made her feel too *easy*. It didn't.

He worshiped her body, taking his time on every inch

of skin.

Kissing, caressing, exploring…

Everything he did was just right, like he knew exactly what to do. Of course he did, because he was in her head. He could feel what she felt, so that took all of the guesswork out of lovemaking.

The experience was unlike anything she'd ever felt before.

For once, she could lie back and completely give herself to another, without worries about repercussions. Or doubts about how he really felt about her.

She'd asked him to make her his. And he was doing just that.

With his fingers circling her nipples, making them stand to attention, begging to be touched some more.

With his lips, which left a trail of kisses down from her cleavage and belly button right down to her most intimate parts.

She spread for him.

He applied just the right amount of pressure to her clit with his thumb, teasing her entrance.

God, she was wet.

It was a revelation, how he played her so effortlessly.

She closed her eyes squad and found that she could see what he saw. He dove down, pressing his face against her curls and tasted her like no man had ever done before.

Sure, she'd had sex; she'd even had the odd partner go

down on her. But those attempts had been clumsy at best. Thomas was a master at work.

Jill cried out, then covered her mouth with both hands.

Tears of happiness stung in her eyes.

Thomas pulled away from her, leaving her painfully exposed.

She couldn't take it.

My turn, she thought.

He sat at the foot of the bed on all fours, waiting.

She got onto her knees and wrapped her arms around his neck, kissing him deeply. He tasted as sweet as he did before, with a hint of her own scent on his lips.

He held on to her around her waist as she straddled him.

What a beautiful specimen he was. Chiseled abs. Just enough hair peppering his chest to make him look manly.

And those arms. He could lift her up like it was nothing.

Jill lifted one of her legs, allowing her hand to slip underneath.

His cock was rock solid. She wrapped her fingers around his shaft and squeezed. It felt like pure energy. Pure pleasure.

She wanted it; she wanted him.

I want you too, he thought.

There would only be one first time, and perhaps she should have held out a bit longer to enjoy the tension, but she couldn't take it anymore. In any case, could it get any better than perfection?

Jill let go of him and lowered herself onto his lap. It had been a while for her, and she felt her tight muscles struggling to let him enter. It stung slightly, but it was a sweet sort of pain.

And soon, they were one.

It wasn't just a physical thing which she felt. Her feelings deepened as well.

The entire experience was indescribable.

She rode him, rocking against him gently at first until she found the perfect rhythm. He spurred her on with his hands digging into her hips.

Her mind filled with all the imagery *he* saw.

The way her lips parted slightly every time she exhaled.

The tiny beads of sweat on her brow, as well as on her cleavage.

These were the little things he noticed, though his perception was fuzzy at best.

She saw little things too.

The way his muscles flexed as he supported her ever more feverish movements.

The little crease that formed between his eyebrows, signaling that the finish line was in sight for him.

Before Jill knew it, she felt it too. A wave of warm, sticky-sweet goodness enveloped her from the inside out. A million butterflies seemed to collect in her lower abdomen, ready to burst through.

She was so tense she could explode, and at the same time, a peace descended over her which she'd never known before. Like a shaman having an out-of-body experience, she felt like she was starting to float and look down on the two of them.

Then, as he started to shudder and tremble with the onset of his orgasm, she was pulled back in a flash.

All she could see was bright white stars. And a pair of eyes. His eyes.

The blue depths drew her in, and made her feel safer than she'd ever felt before.

Her release washed over her, leaving her body and mind limp as well as sated.

It was done.

She was spent.

He was hers. And she was his.

———◆———

Come morning, Jill found herself in an all too familiar setting. In bed, staring up at the ceiling in the dark.

But this time her heart wasn't filled with regret anymore. She wasn't plagued by unwanted fantasies that tried to arouse as much as they frustrated her.

This time, she was completely at peace.

She reached for the arm draped across her waist—Thomas's arm—and squeezed it as if to reassure herself that he wasn't just a figment of her imagination.

No, this was all real.

Jill sighed contently and rested her head against his shoulder.

Although this story had started many months ago, when she'd first laid eyes on Thomas as he arrived on base, all the action had only started to happen during this past week.

How much they'd been through, in such a short time…

Was that why she felt like she'd known him forever?

What a crazy start they'd had together. After avoiding each other for six whole months, they'd come together in a most spectacular fashion. Their love story had it all. Drama, conflict, heartbreak, and now, a happily ever after.

She felt complete. Her life wasn't missing a man as Lauren had suggested. It was much more complex than that. She had lacked passion, companionship.

She'd been on her own for so long she didn't know how good it could feel to have a support network to fall back on. To have one person in her life who would do anything for her.

For all his flaws, which, in fairness, he'd tried to overcome during their brief time apart, he *was* loyal. And she couldn't fully understand how it worked or why it had happened. But he'd chosen her.

Or fate had.

Somehow they'd ended up together.

She'd heard his thoughts, felt his innermost desires. He

would move heaven and earth for her if necessary. Earlier she'd wished that he would have chosen the squad over his uncle's selfish instructions, and now she realized he'd made his final choice. His loyalties lay with *her* now, not the squad.

The way she felt about Thomas now didn't leave room for any more doubts. The bond was rock solid. She was certain that after everything they'd overcome together, nothing would come between them anymore.

Would they tell their children about all of it one day? Could they even *have* children? Jill wasn't sure, but she couldn't wait to find out what the future would have in store for the two of them.

And the squad, of course.

Because no matter what went on between the two of them, they were still a part of something else that was bigger than just the two of them.

They would always be part of Alpha Squad.

And when the alarm on her phone went off, she'd sneak out of his room, down the hall, and start a brand new day on the job. And this beautiful thing she had with Thomas Blackwood would remain a secret. At least for now.

- THE END -

ABOUT THE AUTHOR

Dear Reader,

Thanks for reading Alpha Squad: Infiltrator. This is the third book in the Alpha Squad series, which serves as a spin-off to my well received Scottish Werebears series, which came out in 2015-2016. If you enjoy Vampire Romances as well, you might also want to check out my Vampires of London series in which I currently have three titles out; Alexander's Blood Bride, Michael's Soul Mate and Lucille's Valentine.

I may have only released my first book in 2015, but I'm not new to writing in general. In fact, my mom still tells me to this day about how I would make up stories, and attempt to record them in my clumsy, shaky handwriting from the moment I learned to read and write. From there I went on to write fan fiction and other stuff meant for my own eyes only.

I've always enjoyed stories of the paranormal. Vampires, shape shifters, witches and magic, all featured in the books I loved the most, even when I was still growing up. But it wasn't until much later that I got into romance. One of the first writers (a self-published author just like me!) I came across was Tina Folsom, via her Scanguards Vampire series. I was hooked. From there I went on to read more paranormal romance until I found a new kind of hero I loved: bear shifters, like the kind written by Milly Taiden, Zoe Chant, and T.S. Joyce. What I love about bears is how they can be all strong and independent, a bit reclusive, and almost grumpy, but they always end up having a heart of gold (plus they tend to know their food, and we all know that a man who can cook is doubly sexy). All that (except for the shifting into a powerful bear) almost exactly describes the sort of man I ended up falling for and marrying in real life, so it's no surprise that this is what I started my publishing career with.

To find out more, check:

LoreleiMoone.com (And why not sign up for the newsletter to be the first to find out about new releases.)

You can also get in touch with me via Facebook (search for Lorelei Moone), or email at info@loreleimoone.com

x Lorelei

HAVE YOU MET THE SCOTTISH WEREBEARS?

Before there was Alpha Squad, there were the Scottish Werebears... And if you sign up for Lorelei Moone's mailing list at loreleimoone.com, you get Book 1, Scottish Werebear: An Unexpected Affair absolutely free!

Titles in the Scottish Werebears series include:

An Unexpected Affair

A Dangerous Business

A Forbidden Love

A New Beginning

A Painful Dilemma

A Second Chance

These individual books in the Scottish Werebears series are best read in order. They can also be enjoyed as part of the Scottish Werebear: Complete Collection boxed set.

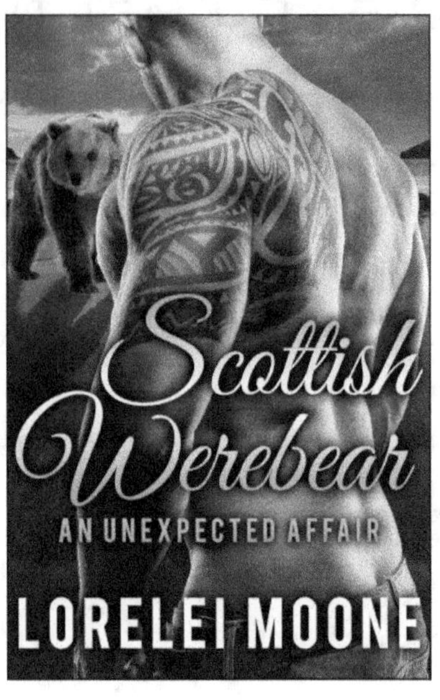

When romance novelist, Clarice Adler, hides herself away in a secluded holiday cottage to finish a book, the last thing she needs is another relationship. Imagine her surprise when she falls head over heels for the man who runs the place. Derek McMillan knows Clarice is his mate, but he's a bear shifter and she's human and the two simply don't mix. They are literally worlds apart; can they find a way to come together?

Get this book for free by joining Lorelei Moone's mailing list at loreleimoone.com!